THE TRAIL TO REPARATION

PLAINSMAN WESTERN SERIES BOOK FIVE

B.N. RUNDELL

WOLFPACK
PUBLISHING
— EST 2013 —

The Trail to Reparation
Paperback Edition
© Copyright 2022 B.N. Rundell

Wolfpack Publishing
5130 S. Fort Apache Rd. 215-380
Las Vegas, NV 89148

wolfpackpublishing.com

Paperback ISBN 978-1-63977-800-3
eBook ISBN 978-1-63977-799-0

Kids. What a blessing they can be and what a challenge. But life is all about growth and when you wake up one day and find your kids are grown and gone, we get a little melancholy and reflect on those days of blessing and challenge. Then, we remember that one time, not so very long ago, we walked in those shoes, and we were the blessing and the challenge to our parents. But through it all, we finally begin to learn that each and every day can be a blessing or a challenge, but each day will pass into memories, and we can treasure each one, whether diamonds, emeralds, or simply shiny stones, each a treasure of its own. So, I dedicate this work to the many blessings, children, grandchildren, and yes, great grandchildren. Maybe someday, they might read these words and know they, each and every one, were a very beloved blessing.

THE TRAIL TO REPARATION

1 / SANGRE

The big Sharps rocked Reuben back on his knee as it roared, bucked, and spat lead. Two hundred yards away across the dry grassy valley bottom, a young bull buffalo stumbled and fell on his bearded chin, the black wooly head twisting to the side as the massive brown hump seemed to drive the mound of matted fur and muscle into the deep grass, slowly falling to the side and with one last grunt and a groan of exhaling breath, the beast of the wilderness gave its last bit of life to the hunter.

"That's meat!" declared the blonde-haired blue-eyed woman that stood behind her man, dropping her hand to his shoulder. Reuben glanced back at his wife, Elly Mae, as he jacked the lever of the Sharps down to open the breech and reload the .52 caliber rifle, the weapon that had seen him through his time with Berdan's Sharpshooters in the early years of the war between the states. The rifle was as much a part of him as anything he owned for it had given them meat and protection through the early years of their life together, years spent as deputy marshals recruited by Ben Holladay and Governor Evans to protect the gold

1

shipments on the stage line. But now they were making their home in the shadow of the Sangre de Cristo mountains in south central Colorado Territory, and they needed meat for the coming winter in the high country.

Reuben sat back on his haunches as they watched the rest of the small herd of buffalo slowly meander away from the carcass of the young bull. They were surprised to see the herd of woolies in this high mountain valley, knowing the big herds of buffalo were usually found in the broader expanses of the grasslands beyond the foothills to the east, but the meat from this one beast would be a good start on filling their cold storage basement beneath their newly built log home. Their friend from the goldfields, James Foley, the wily old mountain man, had guided them to this valley and helped them put up the house, convincing them to have a cold storage basement that could double as an escape route if the need arose.

This was their first time to get away from the building of the cabin and get a start on laying up stores for the coming winter. The valley that lay on the east side of the mountain range was about ten miles at its widest and roughly 25 miles long, running north and south below the Sangre de Cristo mountains. A fertile valley with a series of creeks that came from the southern mountains and joined with the many runoff creeks from the high mountains, to merge and flow to the northeast before turning to the west and dropping through the foothills to eventually feed the distant Arkansas river.

"Every time I look at those mountains, I am amazed at the beauty!" declared Elly, sitting beside her man, her knees drawn up to her chest and arms wrapped around them. She glanced at Reuben and back to the mountains. "The colors! From the green of the valley to the splashes of gold of the aspen that crowd the lower ridges and valleys, and the deep red of the oak brush on the foothills, it's so different from the east."

Reuben's childhood was spent in the south of Michigan territory and Elly's was in the farmland of Iowa before her family decided to move to the west. It was by chance that the two met when the Sioux had raided the Mormon wagon train and captured several young women, including Elleanor Ann McGuire who would soon shorten her name to Elly Mae, and they were rescued by the tall blonde stranger that was the scout for another wagon train. But the two fit together like two parts of the same puzzle and it took little time for them both to recognize that Heaven made bond. With the common love for the wilderness, the mountains, and adventure, they had continually grown closer in their short time together.

The long range of the mountains stood like a garrison of soldiers, standing at attention, their tricorn hats erect and dusted with the first snow of winter, watching over the fertile valley below. Black timber draped from their shoulders like starched uniforms hugging the bulging muscles of the almost insurmountable peaks and laying on the creases of the long ridges that stretched like the stiff-legged soldiers they mimicked. The image before them gave Elly an odd sense of security and safety as if they were a barrier between them and any danger that might come their way, but little did she know what lay in store for them.

Reuben leaned his shoulder against hers, "Looks like the rest of the herd has moved away so let's go down and get started. That's gonna be a bigger job than we've tackled before."

Elly smiled, reached over to run her hand through the fur behind the head of the big black dog that looked as much like a wolf as his namesake, and said, "C'mon Bear! We've got work to do!"

Reuben stuffed the Sharps in the leather scabbard beneath the right fender leather of his saddle and swung aboard his big blue roan known as Blue. He leaned down and snatched up the lead of the pack mule, although the recalcitrant beast preferred to walk beside his buddy Blue free rein, but they were traveling over new ground and Reuben preferred to have the mule on a short lead. Elly stepped into the stirrup, hopped once, twice, and swung aboard her leopard Appaloosa, Daisy. They rode from the rocky promontory that held scattered juniper, twisted cedar, and piñon, with scattered cacti, scrub oak brush, and occasional clusters of aspens. Every day had been a learning experience as they explored their new homeland and although this was their first hunting excursion away from the cabin, it certainly would not be the last. Their friend, James Foley, said this was Ute country and the Jicarilla Apache would often make hunting or raiding excursions into this valley. He had encouraged them to make friends with the Ute for they were often friendly to the intruding white men, and they could try to befriend the Apache, but added, "that might be a little more difficult, especially when they're deter-mined to take yore scalp!"

They had chosen what Elly described as an "island of black timber and foothills" for their cabin and had spent the last several weeks making the wilderness isolation their home. With the cabin tucked back in the trees on a slight shoulder and saddle between the higher timbered knoll and the lower one that lay to the west of the high point, they overlooked the long valley, but the cabin was not easily seen from below. A rocky outcropping behind the cabin also served to hide the escape route that had been dug out from the regular basement to make a cold storage room and route to the back exit that was obscured by thick scrub oak and rocks.

The two-room cabin was spacious by wilderness standards with the main room having a cooking fireplace on the east wall, a broad covered porch on the south that held the door and a window, and the second room on the west side with a window to the west and back side of the cabin that was screened by the thick timber. A loft was tucked in above the second room or bedroom and offered extra room that could be used for another sleeping space or just storage. To the east, they built a solid corral with lean-to and tack shed for the horses and gear, but the animals would spend most of their time in the well sheltered wide meadow in the hollow among the timber covered hills and to the east of the cabin. They used the natural cover and timber to fence off the meadow, with brush and snags filling in the gaps to keep the animals from wandering.

As they neared the carcass, Elly was surprised at the size of the beast. "He is big!" she declared. Reuben chuckled as he stepped down from Blue. "This the first time you been this close to one?"

"Yes! I knew they were big, but up close like this, he's huge!" she stated, shaking her head as she bellied down on the saddle and slid to the ground.

"You think he *looks* big; just wait till we open him up and hafta roll him to get the hide off!"

Bear had bellied down to watch as Reuben used his big Bowie to open up the bull from his tail to his chin.

Steam rose from the innards as he reached into the bloody gore to pull the offal out and cut the liver and heart away from the rest. He lay them aside, tossed some of the trimming to Bear and dragged the rest away from the carcass. A glance to the sky showed turkey buzzards gliding on outstretched wings as they watched the unfolding drama below. Bear came to his feet when he spotted a coyote padding close, but a low growl and a fighting stance warned the four-legged trickster away. Reuben chuckled, "We better get a move on 'fore we get outnumbered by the carrion eaters!"

While Reuben worked on the innards and cuts, Elly used her Flemish knife to start skinning the big beast. When she declared, "That's as far as I can go! How we gonna get the rest of the hide free?" Reuben stood, wiped the sweat from his brow with the back of his bloody hand and smiled at his little blonde woman and said, "Now the work begins!"

———

THEY WERE TWO VERY TIRED PEOPLE AS THEY SWUNG aboard their mounts to start home. After rolling the bull over to remove the hide, and deboning most of the meat, they fashioned a travois for the pack mule and loaded the meat aboard. Once the load was secured, Reuben stood tall, arched his tired back, and said, "I reckon that's over three hundred pounds of meat there!" nodding to the stack on the travois.

As they neared their cabin, Elly looked at her man. "I think I'm too tired to even eat any supper!"

Reuben smiled, nodding in understanding. "And we still have to get that into the cold storage!"

"Oh noo," groaned Elly, shaking her head.

The sun was cradled on the mountain peaks of the Sangres when Reuben and Elly sat on the porch, their feet hanging off the edge as they looked at the slow setting sun casting long shafts of gold across the darkening sky. Elly leaned against her man, dropped her head to rest on his shoulder. "Even though I'm almost too tired to appreciate it, that has got to be one of the most beautiful sunsets I've seen!"

"Well, since we've only got blankets and such, it's good that you're tired, cuz we won't start making our furniture until we have our winter stores laid in and we'll be sleeping on the floor!"

"That's alright. The only beds we've slept in have been in the hotels in the cities, and I've had my fill of cities!" declared Elly, scooting even closer to cuddle up with Reuben.

2 / COMPANY

T he grey line of early morning made silhouettes of the foothills and distant mountains, adding mystery to the cascading hills and deep ravines that marked the land to the east of their new home. The light was off Reuben's left shoulder as he climbed the taller knob that lay to the south of their cabin. His Sharps rifle hung from a sling at his back, the leather case with the binoculars bounced off his hip, and he carried his father's Bible in his hand. He crossed the saddle with the break in the timber and moved quietly through the thick pines and occasional fir and spruce. He had picked out his promontory shortly after they chose the cabin site, knowing this spot would offer him an excellent view of the entire valley as well as good cover with the rocky escarpment and scraggly cedar and piñon that would also give sufficient shelter for his early morning time with his Lord. It had long been his practice to take the early morning for his prayer time and being away from the cabin would also afford Elly her own quiet time.

Reuben took his seat on the flat rock, leaned back against the cold stone, and opened the pages of the Bible.

It was not his usual practice to start at some random page or portion, but the slight morning breeze ruffled the pages and flipped several over before he put his finger on the open page. He dropped his eyes to the fourth chapter of first Chronicles and the last verse on the page, *And Jabez called on the God of Israel, saying, Oh that thou wouldest bless me indeed, and enlarge my coast, and that thine hand might be with me, and that thou wouldest keep me from evil, that it may not grieve me! And God granted him that which he requested.*

Reuben frowned, looked at and read the verse again, and slowly let a smile split his face as he lifted his face to the pale grey of the early morning sky and began to pray. The verse had spoken his burden for he wanted God to bless them in their new home and keep them from all evil and he prayed the scripture asking that God would grant what he requested.

He set the Bible aside and sat quietly, savoring the sounds of the waking day. High overhead he saw the slow drifting form of a golden eagle, wings outstretched to soar on the uplifts that came from the valley and mountainous ridges and ravines. As the morning light stretched across the greenery, he saw the shadowy forms of a small band of elk making their way to water, probably coming from the black timber of the flanks of the mountains. He dug out his binoculars, drew up his knees to use to support his elbows and slowly scanned the valley.

Directly ahead and beyond the few hills and buttes that lay in the dry land between his location and the creek bed, were the scattered remains of his bison kill. Several grounded and bloody faced turkey buzzards were digging at the rib cage while a pair of coyotes fought over the pile of bigger leg bones. A badger had his head buried in the remains of the skull that were left after Reuben hacked out the brains and tongue. He chuckled as he watched the creatures of the valley partake of their leftover feast and moved his glasses further out to get a better look at the elk. They wanted to get a couple elk for their stores and may mount that hunt later today.

He started to move his glasses away from the long-legged royalty of the mountains, but something spooked them, and they scattered away from the creek bed, running toward the black timber at the edge of the mountains. Reuben frowned and slowly scanned the area for the source of the alarm. Two elk had fallen, and three men rose from the brush to quickly go to the downed animals and cut their throats. The buckskin attired hunters had downed the elk with arrows and now stood beside the carcasses, jubilant over their kill and animatedly talking with one another. Two bent to the task of field dressing the animals while the third disappeared behind the brush. Reuben caught a glimpse of the third man moving downstream toward a thicket of cottonwood and guessed the man was retrieving their horses. A moment later he was proven right as the man came from the thicket aboard a buckskin-colored horse and leading three other horses.

Reuben slowly scanned the valley, looking for any sign of more hunters, but seeing none, he returned his gaze to the three with the elk. They made quick work of gutting the elk and loading the quartered meat aboard the horses, most going on the riderless pack horse, and covered the meat with the hides. As they swung aboard their horses, they lifted their arms to greet others that appeared from the trees. Reuben counted another six warriors, some leading loaded packhorses and within moments, the entire hunting party was moving to the north, staying well away from the timber of the mountain flanks.

As the band moved away from the creek bottom, two other warriors came from the thickets, riding fast and gesticulating to the others. The larger group stopped, turned and as the others caught up, Reuben could tell the two were motioning toward the creek and beyond, toward the direction of the hills where he lay. Moving his binoculars back to the scene of his bison kill, he saw even more carrion eaters fighting over the cast-offs and offal and assumed that was what the two others were alarmed about. As he watched, several of the band shaded their eyes from the slow rising sun and looked his direction, but Reuben knew they could see nothing, but perhaps the evidence of the kill and the tracks they left were what was alarming the hunting party. But they turned away and continued on their way, probably to their camp or even their village. Reuben knew this to be the land of the Ute, and maybe their village was nearby.

He continued to scan the valley, searching for game and any other visitors, or hunting parties. They had thought they had come to a land that had few if any residents, even though they knew it was the land of the Ute and possibly the Jicarilla Apache, but they did not think there would be any villages nearby. Another bunch of elk, maybe eight or ten, mostly cows, were further south but still near the creek. They had come for water and were lazily grazing on the deep grass. Several deer had come from the foothills, always in bunches of five to ten, mostly does with their new fawns that had outgrown their spots but not their playfulness as they bounded about showing their endless energy. He started to move his glasses away from the creek when he spotted something different, and he focused in on a family of big-horn sheep. He saw one big ram with more than a full curl, two other smaller rams that were sparring and cracking heads with one another. He counted five ewes and at least that many lambs. It was his first sighting of the big-horns, and he took his time looking them over.

A growling stomach reminded him of his hunger and with a smile and a nod, he finally put away his glasses and rose to return to the cabin. Elly was sitting on the edge of the porch, smiling broadly as she watched him come up the winding trail through the trees to their cabin. She stood to greet him as he climbed the three steps to the porch and embraced his little beauty. They walked arm-in-arm into the cabin as she asked, "So, did you plan out our day for us?"

"Umm, sort of, I reckon. We've got a cold storage room to fill with meat, a stack of wood that needs to get a lot bigger, and an empty cabin that needs furniture, so, where would you like to start, Mrs. Grundy?"

She giggled as she handed him a cup of steaming coffee, and answered, "Well, as far as I'm concerned, I'd rather go hunting any day than to do any of those other chores!"

———

THEY RODE SIDE BY SIDE AS THEY MOVED ACROSS THE DRY flat land toward the greener creek bottom of the valley. As they rode, Reuben told Elly of his sighting of the hunting party of what he assumed were Ute and explained, "We'll have to be especially cautious of any sign we leave, you know, like we did yesterday with the bison. We can't be leaving that much behind to tell others that we're in the area. I think two of those

12

warriors spotted our sign and told the others, but they didn't seem to be too concerned. But we should be careful anyway. If they want to find us it won't be that hard, but no sense in makin' it easy on 'em."

"Is that why we're hunting so far away from the cabin today?"

"Well, yeah, but I did spot some elk up thisaway," he motioned with his chin to the creek bottom and the thickets of willow and chokecherry that bordered the creek and the wide stretches of deep grass that beckoned to the wildlife. "But I think we'll maybe change up our routine, not be predictable as to when and where, just to be on the safe side. On the off days we'll fetch firewood, maybe work on some furniture."

"As far as furniture, the first thing I want us to work on is a table and some chairs!"

Reuben reined up, motioned to Elly to be still, and pointed to the thickets on the far side of the creek. Dark forms were moving slowly among the brush and grassy flats and Reuben knew they were near the elk. He slipped his Sharps from the scabbard and stepped down, looked at Elly and watched as she swung down, her Henry rifle in hand. She went to her knees beside Bear and whispered to him, "You lay still, we'll be back," as she motioned for him to lay down. The big black wolfdog bellied down, but never took his eyes off Elly, watching her every move. The horses were ground tied, the mule staying beside Blue, and the two hunters worked their way a little closer to the creek, searching for a break in the brush to either get a shot or to cross over.

3 / STORES

The thickets of willows and chokecherries were crowded along the creek banks, the chuckle of the creek waters masked what little sound was made by the two hunters. Reuben let Elly take the lead as they waded the shallow waters to move into the brush on the mountain side of the creek. She dropped to one knee to wait for her man as he moved through the grass to come to her side. She smiled, whispered, "Which one should I take?"

"Your choice, but a young bull like that spike out there in the grass would be a good bet, but if you choose a cow, make sure there's no calf," he cautioned, pointing only with his chin, and whispering close beside her. She nodded, turning her attention to the elk that were about a hundred yards away and began to mentally pick her way through the brush. A glance back to Reuben and she started in a low crouch, slowly pushing aside the drooping willows, moving only with the morning breezes that made the grasses look like waves on a lake, and began her stalk. Within a few yards she dropped to all fours and moved under the willows, working her way closer. She knew the Henry was a deadly weapon, but to drop a thousand-pound elk it might take more than one .44 caliber slug in the right place.

At just under sixty yards, Elly stretched out with the Henry held steady, her elbows resting in the soft grass, and narrowed her sight on the spike bull, choosing her target at the small of its neck, just below his ear. Having already jacked a shell into the chamber, she slowly eared back the hammer, knowing the metal click might alarm the animals but it was muffled by the chuckle of the creek and the deep grasses. Her sight picture steady, she took a deep breath, slowly let some out and squeezed off her shot. The Henry responded, jamming the stock back against her shoulder, bucking slightly and barking to send the slug to its target. She instantly jacked another round into the chamber, watched the bull stumble, shake its head, and step off, but her Henry spoke again, and the second slug blossomed red no more than three inches behind the first. The bull lifted its head as his front legs buckled and he fell to his shoulder, kicked his back legs, and lay still.

When Elly eared back the hammer on her Henry, Reuben rose slowly to one knee and took aim at another bull with long spikes and a short stub of a branch on his growing antlers that still held velvet. The chosen bull was just over a hundred yards from Reuben's stance and when he dropped the hammer before the echo of Elly's first shot returned, the big .52 caliber lead from the powerful Sharps took the bull just behind the front shoulder and broke at least one rib on its way to explode the heart. The bull dropped like his legs had been jerked from under him, his chin dropping between his front knees and with one last gasp, the bull came to a perma-nent rest.

Elly grinned as she watched the rest of the herd stretch out and head for the tall timber that skirted the mountains. She twisted around to see Reuben stand and smile at his woman and start toward her as she struggled to her feet. She was breathing heavy as she jacked another shell into the chamber and slowly lowered the hammer. Taking two shells from her pocket, she pushed them into the loading gate and topped off her Henry. As Reuben walked toward her, he also reloaded his Sharps, lowering the hammer on an empty cap lock.

Elly's grin split her face as she looked from Reuben to her downed bull. Reuben said, "That's your first elk, isn't it?"

"Ummhmm, sure is!" she declared, her pride dancing like tiny stars in her eyes. She held her rifle cradled in her arm as Reuben came to her side and put his arm around her. "I done good, didn't I?"

"You sure did! I'm proud of you, but if you keep that up, I'm afraid you'll want me to do the cookin' so you can go huntin'!" he chuckled.

"Not a chance! I've had your cooking and you shouldn't be allowed near a cookfire!"

"Fine with me, but now we've got some butcherin' to do!" He stumbled to the side as Bear pushed his way between the two, prompting Elly to bend down and rub the big black dog behind the ears and talk to him.

"You split 'em open, I'll start skinnin'!" declared Elly, walking beside Reuben to her downed bull. Reuben looked at the animal, shook his head and commented, "Got some good meat here!" He started to lean his rifle on the rump of the bull, but that uncomfortable feeling of jitters up the back of his neck caused him to bring the weapon to his shoulder and turn around to scan the valley behind them. There was movement at the tree line but that was over a mile away and could be the rest of the elk. No other movement showed as far as he could tell, but he still felt uneasy and made another scan along the creek, across the slopes, and near the trees. He could see over most of the willows at the creek and he gave the dry flats to the east of the creek a good look-see, but again, nothing stirred. Elly asked, "What's wrong?" for she too had kept her rifle close as she watched Reuben search their surroundings.

"Prob'ly nothin', but I just had that crawlin up my back, you know, when your hair stands on end because there's something you can't see but know is out there?"

"Ummhmm, and you've never been wrong before." She paused, looking from Reuben to the long slopes that lay between the black timber and the creek, "You split 'em, I'll watch. Then we can swap off while I do a little skinnin' and so on."

Reuben lifted his head in a slow nod, looking over the top of his diminutive woman to scan the trees beyond as he grunted his acceptance of her suggestion. With one last scan, he lay down his rifle and slipped the Bowie from its sheath and began the butchering. As he was moving the sharp tip just under the skin to split the hide, Elly said, "Bear's not comfortable either. See how he's pacing and looking toward those trees?"

Reuben glanced at the big dog then to Elly, "Ummhmm, but we don't have much choice. We've got to get these two elk butchered and back to the cabin. How's about you fetchin' the horses and we'll get this done in record time?"

The hard work of butchering the two big elk did little to dispel the unease that plagued Reuben, and he often stood to look around, fearful of some surprise attack by whoever was out there, Indian, renegade, or outlaw.

Once the carcasses had been skinned and most of the meat deboned and bundled in the hides, they loaded the bundles atop the pack mule and behind their saddles. Reuben scattered the remains, knowing the carrion eaters would easily find them but at least they would not be congregated in one area to attract the attention of others. A glance to the sky told of the ever-present turkey buzzards and ravens, and the appearance of a fearless badger brought Bear to his feet and put him on high alert as he stood beside Elly as her protector. But when Reuben spotted a pair of wolves coming from the timber, he called Bear to the side and spoke to Elly, "You and Bear head on out to the cabin. Take the round about way we spoke of, and I'll catch up soon. I want to make sure those wolves don't try to follow."

―――

"THAT WOMAN HUNTS LIKE A WARRIOR!" DECLARED Yellow Nose, the youngest of the four Mouache Ute that sat their horses in the trees beside the little trickling stream that led from the high mountains to feed the bigger creek in the bottom of the valley.

"She is little and has hair like the Meadowlark!" replied Red Hawk, another of the young men. They were part of a small hunting party from the summer camp of the Mouache Ute under the leadership of Kaniache. They would soon move their camp to the land with hot waters, but they were still in need of meat for their winter season. The leader of this small group of young men that were intent on proving themselves as hunters and warriors, was a respected but young man, Mano Blanca, who was the grandson of the great chief, Quiziachigiate of the Caputa band of Utes.

"They hunt in our land and take meat that belongs to our people," declared Mano Blanca, shaking his head. "We will tell Kaniache. Then we will ask to be the ones to drive them from our land!"

"But Kaniache signed the treaty with Carson at the fort. We are to be at peace with the white men!" protested Red Hawk.

"But that treaty was to keep the settlers from our land and from our hunting lands!" argued Mano Blanca, digging his heels to his mount to lead the small party back to their summer camp in the north end of the long valley of the Sangres.

4 / PREDATORS

Reuben stepped to the left edge of the porch to look to the beginning light of day. The pink tint at the dark horizon faded to the dark underbelly of blue that rose to the heights of heaven where the last quarter of moon hung like a ladle that would scoop up the remaining few sparkling jewels that dotted the darkness. Bear had escaped from the interior of the cabin when Reuben slipped out the door, Bear close beside him. As Reuben leaned on the rail, Bear pushed against him, and Reuben dropped a hand to stroke the head of the big black dog that appeared more like a wolf than any breed of dog he knew. His broad flat head held ears that stood alert while his big jowls held the ever-present drool and often lolling tongue from the friendly face. Bear was all black with only a flash of white on his forehead, his big paws let him move silently over any terrain and his black eyes that seemed to flash orange like a wolf, were ever vigilant. He usually sided Elly, but for some reason he chose to be with Reuben on this morning.

The two denizens of the dark moved silently down the stairs to take the path to Reuben's usual morning vigil and prayer park. Reuben had long ago become comfortable in moccasins, and they allowed him to move as silently as his four-footed friend. This morning his Henry hung from a sling at his back and binoculars were snug in their case at his side. The Bible was cradled in his hand and his long strides matched those of the dog, until at the edge of the trees where the saddle crossing was sparse with cover and Bear stopped suddenly, turning only his head to the east and the lower meadow where the horses grazed. A low growl rumbled in his chest and Reuben dropped to one knee beside Bear and whispered, "What is it, boy, what do you see?" and as he spoke he brought his Henry from his back and held it across his chest, his thumb on the hammer.

Reuben slowly scanned as much of the clearing as he could see from the saddle notch, saw nothing. Even the horses and mule were out of sight, probably taking cover from the cold of the night near the trees and away from the exposed grassy flat where the tall grass moved slowly with the morning breeze. Reuben came to his feet but still in a crouch and hugging the tree line, started toward the big meadow. A glance to the sky showed only the sliver of moon and little light from the slow rising sun.

Bear rubbed beside Reuben's leg as they stayed within the tree line, but close enough to look at the meadow. The pale grass waved, showing the dim moving shadows, but the trees were dark. Movement to the left and Reuben spoke softly, bringing Blue close to the brush interwoven with the trees that made the meadow secure, a low nicker from the gelding told him the horses were restless instead of their usual hip shot stance that would be common if they were snoozing. The leopard appaloosa, Elly's mare, pushed between Blue and the brush fencing, and as Blue sidestepped, movement at his other side showed the dark bay mule. The mule bent his head around to look across the meadow, ears pricked and nostrils flaring as he snorted his concern. Reuben looked toward the far trees but could see nothing in the dim light but another quick glance to the eastern sky showed the band of pink rising and the pale blue giving way for the coming sun.

Blue turned to look with the mule, and he too had ears pricked, and his nostrils flared as he sidestepped. They were watching something moving through the trees and coming around the big meadow toward them. Both the mule and Blue slowly sidestepped, keeping their eyes on the movement, prompting the appy to mimic them. Reuben spoke to Bear, "Something's comin', boy," but as he looked down at his side, Bear was nowhere to be seen. He made a quick look around before turning back to watch the trees in the rising light.

A flash of grey showed through a small break. He tried to follow the image, but his peripheral vision caught another flash of movement, but it seemed to be darker, maybe black. *Was it Bear?* No, it was moving right to left, coming nearer, Bear would be closer by and if moving, going the opposite direction. Again, the horses sidestepped, Blue turning back to look at Reuben as if to reassure himself the man was there. Another movement, closer. Nagging at the back of his mind was the image of the two wolves that brazenly tried to approach them at the downed elk, *Maybe they followed us back!*

Mule stepped forward as if to protect the horses, slowly lowering his head and laying his long ears back, he bared his teeth and brayed a challenge to the predators. Reuben moved to his left, looking for a better opening to see the wolves and if necessary, to shoot. He sidestepped, cautious of his footing, never taking his eyes off the breaks where he had seen glimpses of black and grey. He eared back the hammer on the Hawken, dropped his elbow to touch the butt of his Remington pistol as it set in the holster on his left hip, butt toward his right hand. He breathed deep, squinting to see in the dim light.

A flash of grey showed a big wolf clearing the brush in a long leap, ears back, teeth bared, hackles up as he landed and stopped, assuming an attack stance. His head was lower than his shoulders and hackles, his eyes flashed orange, his teeth dripped drool and his tongue slapped against the yellow canines. He lifted one paw, took a step closer, felt or heard his fellow canine drop to the ground as he too cleared the brush and came to his side. Both wolves were grey, black at their paws and neck, their tails held low as they slowly approached the gathered horses and mule. As they came closer, they began to move apart, their eyes always on the mule who now pawed at the ground and shook his head, baring his teeth and grunting a stifled bray.

Reuben moved closer to the brush, stood beside a rough barked ponderosa, and lifted the Henry to sight on the wolf that was a little closer and was the first one over the brush. As the beast lifted his paw and slowly lowered his head just a little more, Reuben knew he was ready to pounce. With a quick breath, Reuben dropped the hammer on the Henry and the blast from the rifle shocked the stillness of the morning. Birds fluttered from the high branches, a squirrel barked, and the wolf staggered. The bullet took the beast in the high shoulder at the neck, but the animal spun, biting at the wound, before turning back to face the mule.

The big bay mule charged when the rifle sounded, startling the second wolf, who did not turn to flee. He pounced at the charging mule, opening his mouth wide to sink his teeth into his prey, but the big mule dropped his head under the pouncing beast and buried his teeth in the neck of the wolf. The angry mule reared up, lifting the wolf high and shook his head side to side, the grey coated predator seemingly limp. When the mule tossed his head, the wolf tumbled end over end, but quickly came to his feet and spun around to face the mule. Reuben's Henry barked again, the bullet blossoming red on the flank of the wolf, causing him to spin to the side and bite at the nuisance.

Reuben jacked another shell, saw the first wolf starting a stalk on Blue and the big gelding reared up just as the wolf started to pounce. Reuben fired the Henry, dusting the flank of the charging wolf enough to throw off his attack and Blue came down with both front feet, driving them into the wounded wolf. Reuben had jacked another cartridge into the Henry and looked to see the second wolf circling the mule, unsure of what to do but refusing to give up. He shook his head as he moved, growling and drooling. Reuben could not shoot without hitting the mule and he moved to the side, looking for an angle. As the wolf tried to move behind the mule, Reuben fired again and was certain he hit the beast but saw no reaction.

Suddenly black showed at the brush as two more wolves cleared the obstacle to join the attack. Reuben swung the Henry and took a quick aim, squeezed off the shot and saw the first of the black wolves flinch. The second turned his attention to where the shot sounded and glared directly at Reuben and lowered his head in his attack stance and started toward the man. Reuben jacked another cartridge and snapped off another shot, dusting the second wolf. The beast howled at the hit, but quickly turned his attention back to the man. Reuben began to rapid fire, moving his sights from one wolf to another and back again. One grey wolf was down, and Blue was pummeling the body with his front hooves as the mule was targeting the first black wolf.

Black fur smashed through the brush to the left of Reuben, and he swung the Henry that direction, but paused when he saw the white spot on the animal's head, *Bear!* Reuben shook his head and watched as the big dog charged at the wounded black wolf, barreling him over with his big body and sinking his teeth in the predator's throat. The two canines struggled with one another, but Bear refused to release the wolf, growling, and snarling as he shook his head side to side trying to break the wolf's neck.

Reuben dropped the lever to jack another round into the chamber, took aim at the wolf at Bear's feet, but the hammer fell on an empty chamber. He jacked the lever again and glanced down to see the empty chamber as the lever was down. He shook his head and looked up to see another grey wolf coming directly at him. He dropped the Henry and grabbed for his pistol, stepping back from the charging beast when his heel caught on a root of the ponderosa, and he stumbled backwards just as the pouncing wolf seemed to be face to face. Reuben saw the bared teeth, the outstretched paws, heard the snarl and lifted his arm to protect himself. But he was startled to hear the blast of a rifle and saw the airborne wolf twist in the air as a bullet pierced his side. The wolf crumpled beside Reuben who quickly rolled away and came to his feet as another blast came from the trees and the wolf whimpered, tried to get up but a third shot finished the beast.

Reuben lifted his eyes to see Elly holding a smoking

Henry across her chest as she looked at the remains of
the wolves in the clearing. The mule had kicked the one
wolf halfway across the big meadow, Bear stood
astraddle of his conquest, and Blue had stepped back
from his and had dropped his head to watch the lifeless
body. The appaloosa mare was standing further away,
trembling, until she heard the voice of Elly as she came
near the brush fence. Reuben dropped his head, breathed
deep, and reached to pick up his Henry. He shook his
head as he walked to Elly's side, slipped his arm around
her shoulder, and said, "Thanks!" She smiled up at him as
she stroked the head of the appy mare who had stretched
across the brush for her touch.

"Anytime! Just don't make it a habit! I was trying to
fix breakfast!"

5 / WORK

The aspen grove had several standing dead, apparently from some previous drought or the ravages of a nearby fire, but the aspen wood was light and strong, exactly what Reuben wanted for his furniture making. They were on the back side of their mountain that sat like a lone vigil on the east edge of the valley, thickly timbered while further to the east the rough hills were sparsely covered with juniper and piñon, bunch grass and cacti. Much of the aspen grove still bore the golden leaves of fall, fluttering in the least breeze to be true to their name of Quakies. Reuben stepped down, offered his hand to his fair lady and the two began browsing through the thicket, picking out the grey weathered snags they would snake back to the cabin to apply their skills and turn the dead wood into usable furniture.

Bear took off, bounding through the trees as if experiencing freedom for the first time. He made no noise, his passing as silent as the breeze, and soon disappeared into the thicket. Elly smiled as she watched him go, knowing he would return in his own time and she had no need to worry, he was big enough to take care of himself. She gathered up their tools, a bow saw, double bladed axe, hatchets, and the rope for bundling the snags to take them back to the cabin. Reuben had chosen his first standing snag, glanced back at Elly. "I think this one will split and make a tabletop!"

"Suits me, I don't know what to do, so you'll have to be patient," she stated as she walked to his side, looking at the dead tree; all the bark had dried and fallen off, leaving the smooth grey weathered wood. She touched it, felt the texture, and smiled at Reuben. "Too bad it won't be that smooth after you split it!"

"Oh, it'll be smooth when we're done, we'll use some of that sandstone to smooth out the grain and I think you'll like it."

Reuben took the bow saw from Elly and dropped to his knees to start his cut as near to the ground as possible to get most of the big trunk for the tabletop. While Reuben busied himself with the snags, Elly tended to the animals, loosening the girths, picketing them on some grass but close by, and slipping their rifles from the scabbards and standing them at the foot of a lone ponderosa.

When Reuben had a couple trees on the ground, Elly was tasked with delimbing them and bundling the larger limbs that would also be used. The two worked well together and in short order had several logs and bundles ready, but it was also time for a break and some food. With some leftover biscuits and meat, they enjoyed their repast and topped it off by sharing a can of peaches they traded for in Cañon City, the new town on the Arkansas River that had been established as a supply point for the mines in South Park.

Elly was enjoying the last peach, the syrup trickling

down her chin, when Bear came trotting into their midst. He went directly to Elly and rubbed his head against her shoulder, and she relented and started stroking his long fur behind his ears.

"Boy, does he have you trained!" declared Reuben, chuckling at the antics of the big dog. But when Bear growled, Reuben frowned, thinking the dog was growling at him but a quick glance told him the dog was looking well beyond him. Reuben turned quickly to look behind him and saw a bear that had stopped about forty to fifty feet away and was looking directly at them. The bear, a black bear that bore the color of cinnamon with a few blond streaks, slowly rose to its hind feet, trying to get a better look at these intruders. Reuben stood slowly, facing the bear and quietly asked Elly, "Where's the rifles?"

She had also risen and stood to the side and slightly behind him as she answered, "Behind the bear."

Reuben gave her a quick scowling glance and asked, "Do you have your pistol?"

"Don't you?"

"No! I took it off so I could handle the saw! It's over there, where the logs are stacked!" he nodded with his head to the logs that were about thirty feet away, stacked so they could be tied and dragged back to the cabin.

"Well, my pistol won't kill a bear! It'll just make him mad!" hissed Elly.

"He don't look too happy now! Maybe he hasn't smelled the horses yet!" whispered Reuben.

"Uh, given the choice, I'd rather he ate horsemeat instead of me!" said Elly.

The bear dropped to all fours and took a few steps toward them until two smaller versions came bounding from the trees and ran into the side of the cinnamon bear, almost bowling her over. She whirled around, smacked at one and snarled at them both, then with a quick glance to the intruders, she lumbered away, cubs trailing close behind, through the lower edge of the aspen grove.

Both Reuben and Elly let out long breaths, relaxed, looked at each other and started laughing as Elly stepped into the outstretched arms of her man. They embraced as they laughed together, and Reuben said, "Guess that'll teach us to keep our rifles close!"

"Aww, I was kinda lookin' forward to seein' what you would do with your Bowie knife!" declared Elly, giving her man a mischievous smile as she leaned against him.

"I mighta just sliced off a steak from your ornery rump and tossed it to her!"

"Ha! You'd have to catch me first, and remember, when you're in a bear race, all I have to do is outrun you!"

They hugged one another again and Reuben looked down at Bear and asked, "What about you, Bear? I thought you were supposed to protect us!"

"He did. He spotted the she-bear first and told us when he growled," explained Elly, rubbing the black dog's head as she spoke. She looked at him. "Didn't you, boy?" and rubbed him behind his ears as he wagged his tail so hard, he twisted in the middle.

"Well, if we get a move on, we can get these logs back to the cabin and maybe get something made, you reckon?" suggested Reuben.

"Oh, alright. Since you don't wanna go bear hunting, I guess we'll have to go to work!" she answered, smiling as she went to fetch the horses and pack mule.

All the while they worked building the cabin, they made it a point to never drag the logs back the same way to prevent making a trail back to their home. They did the same with the lighter aspen logs, snaking them through the timber and taking a roundabout route to their home. As they dragged the load behind the horses, the pack mule was loaded with several bundles of branches that would be used for uprights and support legs and more and were just as necessary as the bigger logs. When they neared the cabin, they were surprised to see four horses tethered to the rail and four men seated on the porch, their feet dangling over the side, apparently waiting for their return. As they came into the clearing, one of the men stood and lifted a hand. "Howdy, folks! Hope you don't mind; we were waitin' a spell to see if you'd return."

"What brings you fellas to the mountains?" asked Reuben as he stepped down from Blue. He had put his holstered pistol back on his belt and his jacket hung open enough to reveal he was armed.

The speaker said, "Well, we came lookin' for some sign of a mine a friend of ours staked out and told us about. But he neglected to tell us exactly where it was!"

"Ummhmm, and if he wanted you to find it, why didn't he tell you?"

"Well, he up and died on us," explained the man. He looked at Reuben and Elly, then added, "Oh, sorry, ma'am, I'm Si Smith, sheriff of Pueblo County, and this is my brother, Stephen, and that fella," pointing to one of the other men, "is Hugh Melrose, and the other'n is William, Billy, Holmes," he paused, expecting them to introduce themselves.

Reuben nodded, "I'm Reuben Grundy and this is my wife, Elly," and offered no more.

The sheriff continued, "We're up here because a friend of ours, Jim Doyle, a rancher down on the Huerfano, had come into the valley here 'bout a year ago and found some paydirt. He said he spotted a big wide vein that ran down to a creek and the ore assayed out to be one-half pure silver! He told us about it, but then he up and died 'fore he could bring us up here to find it, and well, that's why we're here."

"Here? There's neither a vein nor a creek here!" declared Reuben, motioning around the clearing.

The sheriff chuckled, dropped his head, "No, sir, there certainly is not. But we were crossin' the saddle down below, headin' to Grape creek canyon, and saw the trail and found your cabin. So, we thought we'd ask if you'd seen anything like that?"

Reuben shook his head, glanced to Elly and saw her undoing the packs of branches on the mule, then looked back at the men, "No, nor have we been lookin'. We have no interest in minin' or prospectin'. We're just tryin' to get settled in here as far away from the craziness like what's been goin' on in South Park, as we can get! So, if you gentlemen will excuse us, we've got work to do!" Reuben stood waiting for their response, not wanting to turn his back on any of them. He had seen no evidence of the man being a sheriff and knew it would be an easy lie to try to gain credibility, and anyone that would make themselves to home in a stranger's domain was not someone he was willing to trust. As he looked from man to man, they began to squirm and stand, making their way to their horses.

"We'll be movin' on then. And if you should stumble on the site we described, just remember it's already been filed on and would do you no good to try to take it over," the tone of the sheriff was somewhat of a warning or an attempt to intimidate.

Reuben grinned, "Sheriff, you and I both know that if

that was filed on, it would also have a description of the location and you would not be wanderin' around tryin' to find it!" Reuben shook his head as he lifted his hand to rest on the withers of Blue and watched as the men mounted up to leave.

The sheriff had to add, "That's the problem, his description would fit just about anyplace in this country. It's the markers that make the difference, and we can't find the markers unless we find the claim!" He slapped legs to his black horse and led the others from the clearing. Reuben stepped up on the porch for a slight promontory to watch as the strangers rode from their home, turned on the trail that would take them to the northwest and into the bottom of Grape Creek.

6 / INTRUDERS

He was a little late getting to his morning promontory for his time with his Lord, but he enjoyed looking at the scenery of the early morning. The sun was painting the eastern sky with shades of pink and gold, bouncing the colors high above to tint the under-bellies of the hovering clouds. Instead of the usual cloud-less morning that revealed the azure canopy, the clouds seemed to be gathering over the mountains and valley, perhaps bringing some early snow to the high country. As he finished his reading and the usual heart-to-heart time with his Lord, Reuben leaned back against the big granite stone and propped one knee up to rest his elbow as he savored the sounds of the awakening mountains.

One early riser, a golden eagle rose high on the uplifts, but craned his head down and uttered a scream that Reuben took as a 'good morning' from the amazing bird. In the flatlands below the knoll, a small herd of pronghorn showed their speed as they fled across the uneven terrain without any concern for the rocks and cacti, appearing to sail across the flatland and seldom touch the ground. Something had startled them, and

Reuben slipped his binoculars from the case and searched the flats below his timbered knoll. Three Ute warriors were standing beside the carcasses of two downed pronghorn, laughing and talking with one another before they began the task of dressing out their kills. The men had fringed buckskin leggings, breechcloths, fringed and beaded tunics and their hair was in braids, each with a topknot that held at least one feather, one that had three. One bore a hair-pipe bone choker, two had hair-pipe bone breastplates and the third had ornate beading on the chest of his tunic.

Reuben had heard no rifle shots and assumed the three had taken their game with bows and arrows, which reminded him of his thinking about making a bow or trading for one. It was impossible to take any game without making everyone in the area aware of his presence when he used either his Henry repeater or his Sharps rifle. When he was a young man on the farm, he had traded with some friendly Potawatomie natives for a bow and quiver of arrows, but they got the better of the deal when they dealt him a bow of limited strength and incapable of sending an arrow more than fifty yards and without enough power to drive the arrow through anything but grass. He shook his head at the remembrance and dropped his eyes to the warriors.

One man was gesturing to the west and Reuben lifted the binoculars to search the flats between the two buttes that rose as sentinels beyond the timbered hills where he had built his cabin. As he looked, he spotted a hunting party of about eight or ten warriors moving toward the valley bottom and the willow shrouded creek. As he watched them ride slowly away from the rising sun, he shook his head. *We came all this way to get away from people and we've got more neighbors here than we would've had in Buckskin! Why do they have to be in our valley?* He let a slow grin split his face as he considered his own thoughts, realizing these people and those that were their fathers and grandfathers had probably been in this valley for decades, maybe even centuries!

With a glance to the sky and the gathering clouds, a searching look to the distant mountains to see the first dusting of early snow, Reuben wondered if this was the day when they would get their first snowfall. The air was cool, and the clouds hid the slow rising sun as it painted a silver lining to each one, but the signs were there, and he was thinking snow was coming. He gathered up his Bible, slung the Henry over his shoulder and replaced the binoculars in their case and rose to return to the cabin. He smiled as he thought of Elly, probably finishing the last bit of breakfast makings in anticipation of her husband's return, and the thought quickened his pace. Bear trotted down the trail before him, wagging his bushy tail as he quietly padded through the trees, and both were thinking about the morning meal.

Elly stood in the open doorway, smiling and with hands on her hips as she watched her man and her dog bounding up the trail to the cabin. She never tired of seeing Reuben smile as he neared her, proud that he was as happy to see her as she was to see him. With two bounding steps, he was before her and slipping his hands around her waist as she leaned into his embrace. When they leaned apart and looked at one another, she asked, "Did you tell Him I said Hi?!"

Reuben frowned, looking at her with a questioning expression and asked, "Who?"

She shook her head and giggled, "Who were you just talking to?"

"I was prayin'!" he declared, still wondering at his woman's question.

She smiled broadly, "And did you tell Him I said Hi?!"

Reuben slowly smiled, lifting his head in a nod, and said, "You're s'posed to tell Him that your own self!"

"Oh, I do! But an extra word from someone special never hurts!" she explained as she turned back to the cookfire to gather up her makings. She bent to lift the Dutch oven with the biscuits onto the new table, sat the lid aside, then brought the frying pan from the side rock to sit it beside the table to show off the meat strips and timpsila. She poured the coffee as Reuben took his seat, then she sat opposite her man, and they joined hands to thank the Lord for the blessings.

As they dished up their meal, Reuben said, "Saw some Ute hunters take a couple pronghorn down below the knoll, and some more of 'em headin' towards the creek in the bottom."

"How many?" she asked as she forked out a biscuit from the hot pot.

"Oh, maybe a dozen or so. They were busy huntin'. Prob'ly gettin' in the last of their winter stores."

She started to ask if they had seen him, but she knew if they had he would have told her right off. They had talked about what to do if any of the natives decided to pay them an unfriendly visit, but no matter the plans, each and every encounter would have its own challenges and dangers. "You think they'll get any closer?"

"Hard to say. We haven't seen much game here on this mountain and the surroundin' hills, plenty more in the valley, and they prob'ly know that. I reckon the herd of pronghorn were just movin' through when they were spotted, and the hunters took 'em. But, we can't be too careful, at least until we get acquainted with em and know what they might do, but I think they'll be movin' to the low country for the winter, so maybe they'll be leavin' soon."

"I'd like to meet some, long as they're friendly, and learn from them. After all, they've been living in this country and know it better than anyone," suggested Elly, smearing some honey on the biscuit.

"Ummhmm, but like we found out with the Cheyenne and Pawnee, not all natives are friendly."

"Well, we made friends with the Arapaho!" reminded Elly. It was the Arapaho chief, Little Raven and his women, Red Bear, Running Antelope, and Wind in her Hair, that helped with their wedding as they were wed by the Shaman of their tribe. Their friendship was unique and bound with the exchange of gifts and sacrifices. They had even provided the marriage lodge for the two newlyweds, and both often talked about their time with the Arapaho and hoped to return one day to see their friends.

Reuben nodded his agreement and cautioned, "But we can't assume all natives are willin' to be friendly. If you remember Foley said this was the land of the Ute and the Jicarilla Apache and they were not always friendly."

"Well, we'll just have to look for an opportunity to make friends," declared Elly, nodding her head to emphasize her point.

Reuben smiled at the optimistic ways of his woman and thought about how grateful he was to have such a woman. He finished his meal and leaned back with the coffee cup in his hands, the steam rising before his face, and he savored the aroma. He looked up at Elly, "I think I might go back up on the far hill, see if I can spot the huntin' party. You know, kinda keep track of where they are. Wouldn't want 'em sneakin' up on us and causin' problems."

"Nope, wouldn't want that. But if it's alright with you, I'll just tag along and have a look-see myself!" declared Elly, standing behind her chair, hands on hips and with a glance to the rest of the items on the table. "I'll be ready in a minute while you finish clearing off the table," she declared as she turned her back to him to try to stifle a snicker and a smile.

Reuben looked down at Bear as he lay before the smoldering fire, "Remember this Bear. Women are fine and helpful until you give 'em room, then they get bossy and all that! What're we gonna do boy?"

"Don't look to him for answers, he does a better job of doing what I tell him than you do!" giggled Elly, her broad smile no longer hiding her mischievous intent.

"Let me have a look please," pleaded Elly as they arrived at the promontory that was Reuben's chosen lookout. The flat rock formation offered a sandstone bench and backrest as two large formations appeared as stacked stone. Reuben handed off his binoculars, took a seat and nodded toward the edge of the escarpment that was concealed by the twisted cedar for her overlook. She smiled as she accepted the field glasses and seated herself with her legs crossed to use her knees to support her elbows and steady the glasses. Her first look was across the expansive valley, scan the willow shrouded creek and the grassy flats beyond. She lifted the glasses to view the mountain tops and the first dusting of snow. She smiled, wiggled a little to give comfort, and continued to scan the valley bottom. With a steady move toward the southwest, she paused, frowning, and adjusting the binoculars and whispered to herself, *What, who, is that?*

She lowered the glasses and twisted around to see Reuben moving up behind her, concerned about her reaction. She handed off the glasses and said, "Down there at the far end of the valley, looks like a whole band or village of people coming this way."

Reuben accepted the glasses, bellied down beside her, and began searching for her discovery. They were several miles away, but the large number bore watching. He lowered the binoculars, turned to his side to look at Elly, "I think you're right. Appears to be a whole village of natives, but just who, I can't tell. Could be more Utes joinin' up with these, or maybe the Jicarilla Apache that Foley mentioned. But for all we know, could be some other tribe. Guess we'll just have to wait and see." He glanced toward the sun moving toward midday, and added, "They've got lots of travel time left and if they're joinin' up with the Ute, they might make it 'fore dark."

But the entourage was slow moving, horses dragging heavy laden travois, children scampering about and reprimanded by grandmothers, and most moving casually like there was no urgency. It was mid-afternoon when the mobile village slowed and began making camp almost directly across the flats from Reuben's promontory. To the west of their hills two to three miles, rose a rocky hillock that stood like a forgotten remnant of the days of creation, a lone knob, dotted with rocks and freckled with piñon and cedar. It was in the shadow of that hillock where the camp was made, most of it out of sight from their outlook.

Elly handed off the binoculars and said, "Looks like we're gonna have neighbors!" nodding in the direction of the gathering.

Reuben accepted the binoculars and lifted them for a closer look. "I think they're the Jicarilla Apache that Foley mentioned. Their clothin' is a little different, they have more trade cloth for shirts and such. The Ute we've seen almost always have buckskin." He spoke as he stared through the glasses, "And the women, some have cloth dresses, not like you would wear, but skirts and such." He knew his observation had roused Elly's curiosity and he handed back the binoculars which she eagerly accepted. Bear was beside her and was watching the distant moves of the people, occasionally whimpering as if asking to go visit. Elly reached out a hand to stroke his big head and said, "Not now, Bear. Maybe later we'll pay 'em a visit."

Reuben chuckled, "Oh?"

"Well, it's the neighborly thing to do, don'tchu think?" she asked, still watching.

———

THEY CONTINUED THEIR VIGIL THE FOLLOWING DAY, curious as to whether the village would move on or stay, and for some reason, Elly was pleased to see they were making their encampment, what she could see of it, into more of a permanent settlement or as permanent as the wandering natives were known to inhabit.

Although the fall colors were painting the flanks of the Sangre de Cristo mountains and the lower hills were showing the reds of oak brush and the orange of the cottonwoods, the golds of the higher aspen were resplendent. Elly leaned back and handed off the binoculars and folded her arms across her chest as she admired the beauty of the late season. "It doesn't have the many colors of the hardwoods back east, but there's something special about the golds of the high country that has no parallel."

Reuben lowered the glasses and sat back beside his

woman and replied, "I know what you mean. Maybe it's the framin' of the splashes of gold with the black timber and the snow-dusted peaks, or just the overall surroundin's that seem to strut the magnificence of our Creator."

She smiled as she gave him a sidelong glance and reached out to rest her hand on his shoulder, "And maybe it's the company!" As they talked, Bear lay at Elly's feet until he saw movement and rose to all fours, a low growl coming from his chest. Both Elly and Reuben looked to see what had interested the dog and saw a group of women, carrying baskets and moving among the scattered piñon trees. "What are they doing?" asked Elly, frowning as she watched.

If it were elsewhere, Elly would have guessed the women were picking apples or some other fruit from the trees, but these were not fruit trees. When she saw one of the women take something from a tree and begin picking at it, then put something in her mouth, Elly frowned. "I think they are picking something to eat! Do you know what it is?"

"You know, come to think of it, I did hear some of the men talkin' about piñon nuts and that they are tasty, but small. That must be what they're doin'," replied Reuben.

"Did you see those baskets? From here, they look to be quite extraordinary. I'd like to see one up close."

"You got anything to trade for one? They'd probably be willin' to do some tradin'," suggested Reuben.

Elly smiled, stood, and said, "That's it! I'll get some goods together and we'll see if they would like to do some trading! That's the best way to get acquainted with them!"

They had picked up a few extra trade goods when

they came through Cañon City, and she was certain she could gather enough to make for an enticing trade with the women. Her excitement put an urgency in her step, and she left Reuben behind as she and Bear bounded down the trail to cross the saddle and take the trail to the cabin. Reuben chuckled as she saw her disappear into the trees going down the slope to the crossing. He gathered up his binoculars, rifle and Bible and started after her, not nearly as jubilant as Elly for he knew that the first encounter with a new tribe of natives does not always go as hoped, but he would be at her side, and they would be armed and careful.

He came to the edge of the trees and spotted Elly behind a tall ponderosa, peeking around at something or someone and he went to her side. She whispered and nodded, "They're coming up the trail of the crossing, there by the big juniper!"

As he looked through the thicket of juniper, piñon, and cedar, he saw the group of women working their way up the hill, stopping at every tree and working at filling their baskets. Reuben nudged Elly away from the tree, whispered, "You wanted to meet them, invite them to the cabin to trade."

She looked at her man and down the hill to the women, nodded and slowly stepped from behind the tree to walk into the open area at the crest of the saddle crossing. She hummed as she walked, glancing up at the women as Bear walked beside her. One of the women spotted Elly and called out to her companions, the women gathering together for their own protection as they saw the buckskin attired white woman with hair like the sunshine walking toward them. Elly called out, "Hii3eti'nohkuseic Nii'ooke'!" which is a greeting used by the Arapaho, but also the only one she knew. She did not know that the Arapaho were not friendly with the Apache.

The women frowned and Elly continued to walk their direction. She had learned some sign language from her friends with the Arapaho and now made the sign to say, "I am a friend. I would like to trade with you." She spoke English as she signed, and the women looked at one another until one woman stepped from the group, signed as she spoke in a combination of Spanish and English to say, "Why are you here and who are you?"

Elly understood Spanish, recognized some sign, and answered, "My man and I have a cabin in the woods, there," motioning to the thicker trees where the cabin set out of sight, "and we trade with those who live in this land. We have beads, awls, needles, pots, and more. Would you like to come and see?" motioning with her head to the trail.

The women jabbered among themselves, and the speaker turned back to look at Elly, glanced at Bear and saw movement at the trees as Reuben walked from the trees and waved, but continued up the trail toward the cabin. Again, the women talked with one another, gesturing, and appearing to argue until the speaker again looked at Elly, "Are there others at your cabin?"

Elly was hesitant to let them know there were no others, but she wanted to be trusted and the truth was needed. She smiled, nodded, "My man is a great warrior and hunter. We need no others. Will you come or do you want us to come to your camp?"

The women huddled again, the speaker apparently interpreting, and they came to an agreement that Elly was to later learn was primarily due to their not wanting to share any trade goods with the others until they had the pick of everything. When the speaker nodded and started up the trail, Elly turned to lead the way. The women began to talk and gesture, showing more excitement than fear, and eagerly followed their newfound friend to her cabin and the trade blanket that Reuben was busy spreading out on the ground before the cabin.

Two blankets lay before the porch, Reuben busily taking trade goods from a pannier and a parfleche and spreading them out to display. Beads of several colors and sizes, awls, needles, skinning knives, decorative bells, spools of thread, two bolts of cloth, one cast iron Dutch oven with lid, and a few tin plates. The women stopped and stared at the treasures and started whispering and pointing as Elly motioned for them to be seated and examine the goods. Two women, one that spoke with Elly and another, were about the same age, perhaps all of thirty-five summers, and were older than the others. The younger women were chattier, but respectful of their elders and often asked for guidance.

The leader of the group, Goos-Cha-Da, motioned to the Dutch oven and asked, "What do you ask for the big pot?"

Elly smiled and said, "That is what we call a Dutch oven. It is good as a pot for stews but can also be used to bake biscuits and more."

The woman frowned and her expression said she did not fully understand, and Elly said, "I'll show you," and stood to go into the cabin. She motioned for the woman to join her, and the older woman looked around the circle of women, then boldly stood to follow the white woman. As they entered the cabin, the woman was in awe as she looked around but readily followed Elly to the fireplace as Elly used the hook to lift the coal laden lid to show the baking cornmeal biscuits. Goos leaned forward, looked into the pot with wide eyes and smelled the baking biscuits. She smiled at Elly as she replaced the lid, and asked, "What will you trade for such a wonder?"

Elly thought for just a moment, then asked, "You are skilled at making the hides into leather?"

"I have made many hides, buffalo, elk, deer, pronghorn, rabbit and more. I am known among my people as the one that makes the softest leather," proudly answered the woman. "Do you wish to have leather in trade?"

"No, but I wish to learn about making leather. We have several pelts, buffalo, wolf, elk, and more that must be cured. If you will take the time to teach me, I will trade your skill for the pot!"

The woman's eyes flared, and a slow smile painted her face. She then grew serious, "But it will take much time and I must stay with my people when they return to our winter camp."

"What time you have, if you teach me well, will be a good trade."

Goos smiled. "I will be the envy of all the women in the village!" and turned to go from the cabin.

The other women had been dickering with Reuben and several were quite happy with their trades. Three baskets, two mostly full of piñon nuts, sat beside Reuben and he was signing to the others, still working on trades. But the women were empty handed, and he promised to set aside those items they wanted, and they would return with the requested trades. As Goos-Cha-Da joined the group, they chattered and pointed and without a word to Reuben or Elly, they turned and walked away. Elly was frowning, wondering why there were no goodbyes until Reuben explained, "Oh, they'll be back. They are goin' to get more trade goods, so, we might want to get a bit more stuff out."

Elly noticed several of the goods stacked on the corner of one blanket and she looked at Reuben, eyebrows lifted in a question. He chuckled and answered, "That's what they have chosen for themselves and went back to the camp to get the trade goods."

Elly slowly lifted her head as she smiled at her man, "And they'll probably bring more women and maybe some of the men."

"Prob'ly," he answered, wryly, letting a smile split his face and add a sparkle to his eyes.

"Then you'll need something that the men might like," directed Elly, motioning her man back to the panniers and parfleches that were in the tack shed.

———

MARCHING PROUDLY BEFORE THE WOMEN WERE THREE men, led by one man, obviously a chief, carrying a trade fusil rifle cradled in his arm. With high and prominent cheekbones, his piercing black eyes showed no emotion, his broad nose accented his stoic features. Long braids, wrapped in what appeared to be fox fur, hung over his shoulders and one feather dangled from a topknot. He wore buckskin leggings, a breechcloth, and a trimmed blanket covered his shoulders. The others were similar in appearance and attire, but the confident stride of the one in front separated him from the others.

He stopped before Reuben, who stood with one hand raised, palm forward, as he greeted the man with, "Ya-ta-hay!" It was a greeting used by the Navajo and others and Reuben thought it would be recognized by the leader. The entourage stopped behind their leader and he began to speak in Spanish, "I am Dasoda-hae, war leader of the Llaneros Apache." He paused to watch Reuben's reaction, then continued by motioning to the man to his left, "This is Mano Blanca of the Mouache Ute people, and this man," motioning to the one on his right, "is Cuchillo Roto, my brother."

"I am Reuben Grundy, and this," motioning to Elly, "is my wife, Elly Mae, called Yellow Bird. Welcome."

"Why are you here?" demanded Dasoda-hae, scowling.

"We have come to live here and trade with our friends," explained Reuben, glancing from one to the other of the men. "Your women have already made some trades and want to do more," he nodded to the women that were chattering and pointing. "But we also have some trade goods that might interest you," he added, having noticed the other men craning around to look at the blanket that held two flintlock rifles and several hatchets and knives.

The chief gave a sweeping motion with his free hand, "This land is the land of the Mouache Ute and the Jicarilla Apache. This is not the land of the white man!"

Reuben paused as he considered his response, "I believe the great Creator made this land for all people that would live here and care for the land and the people and animals of this land. We will take no more than we can eat. We will always share with our friends and help our friends whenever it is needed. We have many goods to trade and will have more as time allows."

Goos-Cha-Da, the older woman, stepped beside the leader and spoke in their tongue, motioning to the blankets, prompting the Dasoda-hae to nod his head and motion to the others to go to the blankets to make trade. The two men went quickly to the blanket with the rifles and began touching and examining the weapons until Reuben picked one up and handed it to Mano Blanca, the Ute. His eyes grew wide, and he lifted the rifle to his shoulder to sight along the barrel, then lowered the weapon to look at Reuben. He spoke in Spanish and asked, "What will you trade for this?"

"What do you have?" asked Reuben.

The man dropped his eyes to the rifle, considered its worth, and started to speak, but the one called Cuchillo Roto interrupted, looking at Reuben, "I have a woman of the Mexicans. She is young, but a good worker. She will do as you ask. I only have to beat her a little."

Reuben tried to stifle a chuckle and turned to Elly, "Uh, you want another woman in the cabin?"

"A what?!" she asked, incredulous at the question.

"A woman! He says he'll trade a Mexican slave for the rifle. He says she's a good worker and he only has to beat her a little," he let a broad smile show as he spoke.

Elly shook her head and squinted her eyes at all the men, then motioned for Reuben to come aside to talk. "If she is a slave, she needs to be returned to her people. Ask more about her, and if you think it's right, then trade. We will take her back to her people or send her."

Reuben grinned. "That's what I thought you'd say. I agree," he replied, and turned back to the men. He approached the men by the rifles and asked, "How old is the girl?"

"She is a woman. Young, perhaps," and flashed two hands and another of all fingers, "this many summers."

"How long has she been a captive of your people?"

"She was taken in the time of green-up. The first raid on the village near Taos."

"What else do you have?" asked Reuben.

"I have a good horse!" declared Mano Blanca. She is the color of her hair," pointing to Elly.

"How old is the horse?" asked Reuben.

Mano Blanca held up four fingers, grinning.

"Is she well-broke and does she ride well?"

"Si, si," he answered enthusiastically, looking from Reuben to the rifle that still lay on the blanket.

When the trades were completed, Reuben and Elly stood over their plunder of baskets, water jugs, bowls, fine tanned rabbit furs, two coyote furs, two pair of beaded moccasins, a beaded tunic for Elly, but they were somber as they thought of the Mexican girl that was to come with the returning men.

Reuben said, "That's why I traded for the horses, I knew the girl would need one and we can always use a spare pack horse. Of course, that man wasn't too keen on the idea of two horses instead of one, but between the two of them, they were happy. To have a rifle among their people puts them in good standin' with the others."

"Do you think the bow you traded for will suit you?" asked Elly as she repacked the remaining goods in the pannier.

"We'll just have to wait and see. He said it was a strong bow made of alder and willow, so we'll have to give it a try." He glanced to the lower trail and said, "Here they come."

THE GIRL WAS PRETTY AND PETITE, ALTHOUGH A LITTLE dirty. Her tattered dress had failed to last even the summer and it appeared she had been given little but rags to cover her. Her head hung and her hair was a tangled mess, but Elly could see she was probably fourteen or fifteen, but badly beaten down. Elly went to the girl, reached out to put her arm around her, but scared eyes caused the girl to lift her arms in a defensive posture and pull back. But Elly spoke softly and encouraged the girl in Spanish and led her to the cabin. As they disappeared inside, the men finished their deal and Reuben took the bow, quiver of arrows, and two horses, shook the men's hands and watched as they proudly carried off their new weapons. Reuben had included some powder and lead balls and gave them a brief lesson on loading and more, but the men were anxious to return to the camp with their treasures and quickly departed, chattering with one another as they took the trail through the trees.

Reuben watched them go, turned and started to the house, but as he started to open the door, he was admonished, "NO! Don't open the door!" He froze in place and asked, "What's goin' on?"

"She's getting a bath!" declared Elly and Reuben heard the two women mumbling together and a little giggle escaped the pair as Reuben sat in the chair with Bear beside him. He dropped his hand to the big dog's scruff and said, "Well boy, looks like we've been exiled!"

9 / SCOUT

"It is as you said, the camp of the Mouache is further up the valley, the camp of the Llaneros Apache is closer and smaller," reported Little Owl, scout for the *Yaparʉhka* Band of the Comanche people.

"How many lodges?" asked the war chief, Piarʉ Ekarʉhkapʉ, or Big Red Meat.

"The Apache have three times two hands, the Ute two hands more."

The chief glanced to his medicine man, Isatai, "And our medicine is good?"

"My vision showed a great victory, many captives, many horses," answered Isatai.

The war chief, a man with great experience in leading raids and mounting war against their enemies had recruited many warriors for this last raid of the season before the snow would fall. He turned to look back at the anxious warriors, young and old among them. He led more than a hundred warriors, each seeking honors and even a new woman for their lodge to warm their blankets during the winter. The young men, a handful on their first raid, sought to prove themselves both in battle

54

and in taking captives and stealing horses. Their eagerness gave needed urgency and spirit to the others that had already proven themselves and wore the scars and feathers to prove their valor and courage.

A quick glance to the rising sun off his right shoulder told the chief it was time. He turned to one of his men, "Black Horse, you take four hands of warriors and hold to the tree line, there," motioning with his chin to the foothills at the eastern edge of the valley, "with the sun on your right shoulder. You will attack the Apache camp when you see White Knife attack. Wolf Killer, you take four hands of warriors, keep to the tree line at the base of the mountains," nodding to the black timber that skirted the big mountain range on the west edge of the valley. "Wolf Killer, follow our lead, we will go for the Mouache!" He stretched his lance high overhead and motioned for all to move as instructed.

After the two smaller bands moved away, Big Red led the others on the west edge of the creek that wound its way through the valley bottom. He motioned to Tosahwi or White Knife, to come alongside. "You will take four hands of warriors, and lead the attack on the Apache camp." The chief knew it would take four fingers of time for his band to get into position for an attack on the Mouache and wanted the two assaults to be simultaneous. Since the Mouache and Jicarilla were allies, if they were to join forces before the Comanche had made their raid, they had the numbers to mount a strong defense, but divided, they could be defeated.

———

REUBEN HAD FINISHED HIS USUAL MORNING TIME WITH THE Lord and reading his word. He took his normal scan of the valley and seeing nothing different from the typical wildlife, he sat back to enjoy his time of reflection and enjoyment of the magnificence of God's creation. A glance over his shoulder to the rising sun told him it was still early morning with the big fireball barely above the rolling foothills and still stretching long shadows from short trees and hilltops.

There was little activity from their new neighbors, the Apache, other than the usual stirring of women fetching water and starting the morning cookfires. He smiled as he thought of the anticipation shown by Elly after just one visit from Goos-Cha-Da, her new instructor in the ways of tanning hides. They started on the wolf hides, there were six of them and they would make great blankets for the coming winter and would also be used to make winter coats. He was somewhat surprised that Elly was so eager to learn this task that was not only difficult, but quite messy, but there was no understanding the ways and wiles of a woman.

At almost first light, he had seen a native warrior riding through the valley toward the south end, but a lone rider was nothing to be alarmed about. He was too far away to tell if he was Ute or Apache, but he was not concerned and had dismissed the thought almost immediately. Now he watched a slow-moving herd of elk making their way back to the black timber and noted the size of the herd showed the bulls had been assembling their harems.

His stomach told him it was time for breakfast and Reuben stood, picked up his rifle, stuffed the binoculars in the case, and with his Bible under his arm, he turned away from the vista, motioned for Bear to lead the way, and stepped toward the trail back to the cabin. He had no sooner entered the trees, than the herd of elk spooked and headed to the tall timber, escaping from the band of Comanche warriors. But there was no alarming sound, no disturbance on his side of the valley, to cause any concern on the part of Reuben, besides, he was hungry, and a hungry man is single minded.

Elly met him at the door, reached up to give him a warm kiss and leaned back to look at him. "So, did you come down from the mountain to see me, or because you're hungry?"

Reuben grinned, chuckled, and put a finger beside his head and said, "Hmmm, let me think about that?"

"Oh you! If you came to see me, I'll feed you. But if you're only hungry, go scrounge up some jerky or pemmican or something!" She answered, pretending offense as she turned away and stomped toward the fire-place, motioning to the newest resident of their cabin, Estrella Esquibel, to fetch the breakfast makings.

Reuben pulled his chair to the table, reached for the coffee pot, and poured a cup of the steaming brew, taking a deep whiff of the delightful aroma that alone pleased him and reminded him of years gone by when he was at home on the farm with his brothers, getting ready to work the fields. When Elly sat the plate full of gravy-covered venison strips and cornbread biscuits, he escaped his reverie and grabbed a fork, but was stopped by Elly. "You just hold your horses, husband! You wait for us, and we'll thank the Lord together!" she declared as she sat down, motioned for Estrella to take a chair, and reached across the table to take Reuben's hand and Estrella's hand.

Reuben grinned, donned his most sheepish expression, and accepted her hand and bowed his head to pray. After giving thanks to the Lord for the day, the food, and

His many blessings, he gave a hearty "Amen" and quickly got on with the day's first business.

He had barely made a dent in the bounty on his plate when Bear came to his feet and growled at the door. A scream came from outside and Reuben vaulted to the door, snatching his Henry as he opened the door to see a panicked Goos-Cha-Da, running toward the cabin. She waved and shouted, "COMANCHE! They are attacking the camp!"

Reuben turned to Elly, "I'm goin' up to the point!" as he replaced the Henry and grabbed the Sharps. He motioned for Goos-Cha-Da to come into the cabin as he slipped his possibles pouch with the ammo for the Sharps over one shoulder, the field glasses case over the other, and said to Elly, "Get your rifle, but all of you, stay here!" He looked down at Bear and ordered, "You, stay!" and shut the door behind him as the big dog scratched at the wood.

He started at a run, down the short trail to the saddle and with a quick glance toward the trail to the Apache camp, ran across the open space and took the tree covered trail up to his lookout point. Once there, he searched around for anyone, friend or foe, and saw several riders coming from the far side of their big hill, charging toward the encampment. Others had attacked from the valley bottom and intermittent rifle fire could be heard among the screams and war cries.

Reuben dropped to one knee and lifted the glasses, scanning the pandemonium of attackers and villagers. The attacking warriors were vicious in their attack, showing no preference between warriors and women, shooting them with rifles and arrows, driving lances through the fleeing figures, tromping on them with their horses, some dismounting and taking scalps and other plunder. It was sudden and catastrophic, bloody, and violent, as death stalked from wickiup to wickiup.

Reuben lifted his Sharps, focused in the telescopic sights and chose a target. A warrior was charging with a lowered lance, chasing a fleeing woman that held a baby in her arms, and Reuben squeezed off his shot. The bullet took the warrior in the side, just below the shoulder and drove him off his mount, to tumble into a morning cookfire, screaming as he fell. Reuben jacked down the lever to open the breech and seated another paper cartridge, lifted the lever, and placed a cap on the nipple, earing back the hammer as he lifted for another shot. His target was a Comanche warrior that dropped from his mount, tomahawk lifted as he grabbed at another woman, but before the hawk fell, the lead from the Sharps blossomed red on his chest, shattering the bone hair pipe breast plate, and driving through the man's chest, exiting out the back to splatter blood over the painted markings on his horse. The animal reared up, pawing at the air, and came down at a run, fleeing the mayhem.

Most of the battle was beyond the butte and out of sight, but not the hearing, of Reuben. Already some of the warriors were leaving the fight, women captives belly down across the withers of their mounts, as they drove stolen horses before them. The sound of the battle was lessening, and there were no other visible targets for Reuben. He stayed on his lookout, rifle at the ready, searching for any target that would even the odds or help his neighbors in any way, but there were none, until finally the victors started en masse from the bloody scene, driving the rest of the horses and a bunch of captive women, some carrying children. There were at least thirty to forty warriors that Reuben could count, too many for him to try to take alone. He watched for a few moments longer until the band of victors and vanquished were moving through the grass beside the distant creek, at least three to four miles away.

He shook his head, replaced the field glasses, and rose from his rocky bench and started back to the cabin. He knew Elly was not going to like what he would have to tell her, but she deserved the truth. He walked slowly down the trail, started across the open saddle, and was stopped by tracks. Tracks of several horses and some afoot. He glanced up the trail toward the cabin, saw the tracks take to the trail and took off at a run. His mind was racing, wanting to cry out for his woman, but not wanting to give away his presence in case there were other Comanche there. He ran through the trees, searching through the openings and burst into the clearing, rifle in hand, cocked and ready, but there was nothing.

"ELLY! ELLY!" but there was no answer. "BEAR! Come here boy!" Nothing moved. He took the steps in one leap, drove through the door, but the emptiness hit him like a wave of blackness, knocking him to his knees. "Elly, Elly, Elly..." he whimpered, knowing there would be no answer.

10 / ALLIES

Reuben stood, looking around, saw Elly's rifle was missing but his Henry still hung above the door. He heard scratching at the door and opened it to find Bear limping into the cabin. He favored his right foreleg and blood showed above his right ear. He had been struck, perhaps with a tomahawk or lance, maybe kicked by a horse, but he was still game. Reuben went to one knee beside the big dog. "We've gotta find her boy, I'll help you all I can. Let me see your leg here," and felt the length of the leg. It wasn't broken, and the blood had dried both on the leg and his head. The dog flopped to his belly, breathing heavy, looking sad eyed at Reuben. "You know what happened, don'tcha boy. But we're gonna get her back. You lay there while I gather up my stuff." Reuben went to the shelves and found the canister of Elly's special salve made from the birch buds, spruce sap, and more and applied a thick coat to both Bear's wounds. The big dog watched Reuben but did not flinch as he ministered to him.

With a packed parfleche with food and extra ammo, his bedroll and a spare blanket, Reuben stepped from the house, dropping the Henry, parfleche, and bedroll on the porch. He ran to the meadow that held the horses, caught up Blue and Elly's appaloosa, unwilling to trust the new horses for this expedition. Leading them back to the cabin, his long stride bid the horses to trot behind him to keep up. As he crossed the clearing, he saw blood sign that told of at least one, perhaps more that were shot by Elly. Once at the cabin and tack shed, he saddled both horses, leaving the girth on the Appaloosa a little loose. He slipped his rifles in the respective scabbards, tied down the saddle bags and his bedroll, put the parfleche behind the saddle on the appy, and returned to the porch for Bear. "Alright boy, we're ready. You comin'?" and motioned with his hand for the dog to follow. Without hesitation, Bear rose and trotted behind Reuben, standing beside the big Blue gelding as he mounted, and when they started off, he fell in beside them.

Reuben dropped off the saddle crossing, choosing the trail that would take them near the encampment of the Jicarilla Apache, curious as to their losses. As he neared the edge of the encampment, three warriors rode out, brandishing their lances and bows, shouting, and screaming war cries. Reuben reined up, holding up his hand in the sign of peace and recognized the warrior leader Dasoda-hae. The leader called the others down, riding toward Reuben alone and held his hand up, palm out toward Reuben.

"Dáanzho!"

Reuben answered with the same greeting, "Dáanzho."

"Ha'déé' ańdéé, What are you going to do?" asked the war leader.

"I'm goin' after them! They took my woman, the Mexican girl, and Goos-Cha-Da."

"You are but one! Did you see the others?"

"What others?"

"The ones that attacked the Ute village. They rode after those that hit our camp maybe two fingers of time later. There were many more of that group. They took many captives and horses from the Mouache."

"Are you or the Mouache goin' after them?" asked Reuben, anxious to get on his way.

"We will wait to see if the Mouache come and join them. The Comanche," spitting the word, "were many more than we had and the Mouache. But perhaps together we can go after them to get our women and children back."

"How many captives did they take?"

"This many women," holding up eight fingers, "and this many young," holding up four fingers. "They also took two double hands of horses." He paused as he struggled with his anger and sorrow, . "They killed this many," holding both hands, all fingers extended, "warriors. But we found more Comanche killed by our people!" he growled in vengeful satisfaction.

"I am goin' after them. I will stay on the high side of the foothills," pointing to the rolling hills that sided the valley to the east, "and I have two horses. I will keep ridin' through the night until I find them."

"And what can you do against so many?" asked Dasoda-hae, skeptical of this white man.

Reuben grinned, "I have fought that kind of battle many times. I will kill them all if I have to, but I'm gettin' my woman back!" declared Reuben. "If you and the Mouache come, let the leader of the Ute know who I am and where I will be. No sense us fightin' each other." The war leader nodded, pulling back from the man as Reuben slapped legs to the blue and started on his way.

Reuben let Blue have his head and the gelding was anxious for the trail; he had plenty of time in the meadow and he enjoyed being on the move. The appaloosa was well experienced at keeping pace with the bigger Blue and often took to a trot to come close alongside as the trail allowed. Following the trail of the Comanche required no effort with so many horses, both ridden and stolen, churning up the soil and grasses. Reuben leaned down for a closer look and could tell by the sign the Comanche were moving at a fast pace, but he didn't expect that pace to continue and within a couple miles, it was evident they slowed. Several of the captives were walking which Reuben was puzzled about, for there were many horses that were unridden. He shook his head, thinking it had to be a ploy of the captors to punish or control the captives, perhaps tire them into submission.

It was shortly before midday when Reuben left the Apache, and he kept a steady pace, alternating from a canter to a trot to a walk and back again, and guessed he had covered about twelve to fifteen miles after a little over two hours. The long valley that lay below the Sangre de Cristo mountain range stretched for about thirty plus miles northeast to southwest. From Reuben's cabin, it was over twenty miles to the south end where the trail of the Comanche pointed. He had been this way only one time, hunting meat for the winter and had seen some straggling buffalo that appeared to be migrating to the south, following the lay of the land that split the finger ridges and foothills from the Sangres and the timbered hills of the Wet Mountains.

Reuben looked to the side to see Bear, trotting alongside Blue, tongue lolling but moving as if he had never been hurt. As they neared the south end of the valley, he saw the trail of the Comanche bore to the southwest, pointing toward the split between the mountain ranges, and was certain they would leave the valley through that notch. He needed high country, he wanted to see where they were and where they would camp. The sun was wasting no time as it settled to the west and would soon touch down on the high peaks of the mountains. Blue was lathering under the breast collar, and he pulled to a stop. As he stepped down beside the narrow creek, he stripped the gear from the horses and let them have a good roll. He let the horses crop grass and get a good drink as he and Bear buried their faces in the creek slightly upstream from the horses.

He stood and stretched, watched as the horses rolled again, stood spread legged and shook before eating more grass. Reuben shaded his eyes as he scanned the lower end of the valley and the end of the Wet Mountains that were his goal. He remembered going into the timber after an elk that got away, but it gave him a look at the flat-topped ridge that rose to the peak at the end. He grinned as he remembered the peak and knew that would be the best place to get a view of the trail of the Comanche, but he had to get there before full dark.

He saddled the horses, both turning to look at him as he dared to burden them again, but they stood and accepted their gear. He swung aboard the appaloosa and Blue looked at him like he had lost his mind, but without hesitation, Reuben dug heels to the appy stretching out the lead with Blue and started toward the long flat ridge that climbed to the top of the lone timbered mountain that stood in the shadow of the taller mountains at the end of the Wet Mountains but overlooked the valley of the headwaters of the Huerfano river.

He pushed the appy hard, and the little mare

stretched out, glad to be in the lead, and took to the steady climb like a true mountain bred horse. Reuben was trying hard to focus on the terrain and the possible ways to attack the Comanche to gain the return of his woman, but images of his Elly crowded into his mind with war-painted warriors around her and mis-treating her. He did not know if she was a captive of a single warrior or if she was just one of the bunch of captives, but his imagination was probably worse than reality, and he shook his head to free it of the violent images. Each thought added fuel to the fire of his rage, and he struggled to control his wrath, but he also knew that if his Elly was hurt in any way, the Comanche would pay in blood. And the words of the Lord came to him in the voice of his godly mother, *"Vengeance is mine, I will repay, saith the Lord!"* And he remembered the first part of that same verse that said, *"Avenge not yourselves, but rather give place unto wrath:"* And his angered mind answered, "Yeah, I'll give place unto wrath alright, just wait till I find one o' them devils in my sights!"

11 / SCOUTING

R euben bellied down atop the lone timber covered mountain that sided the valley of Muddy Creek. With the binoculars held tight, he shaded the lenses with a thick piece of buffalo hide he carried for just that purpose. He was east of the draw and the sun was rapidly lowering above the peaks of the Sangres and the blaze of old Sol was bending swords of gold across the valley and shining almost directly at the prone figure of Reuben. Bear lay beside him, panting from the long run but also watching the miniscule figures below.

The Comanche were making camp and starting several cookfires, preferring to have no fires showing after dusk to give away their location, even though a blind man could follow their trail right to their camp, but it was the way of the people. Their chosen camp lay in a half-moon park with the open end at the creek bank. Stretching about a hundred fifty yards to the arch of the half-moon and about two hundred yards wide, it was a well-chosen site, good cover all around, but also an accessible site if approached through the trees. As Reuben scanned the camp, he saw most of the captives had been herded together just inside the tree line and would probably be tied together or to the trees. Yet there were several that were watched closely as they prepared the food for the warriors and Elly was easily seen with her golden hair showing in the light. A big warrior stood close by, probably barking orders to the white woman as other warriors watched over their charges. Reuben ground his teeth, his cheek muscles rippling as he breathed heavily and slowly shook his head. He knew he had to stifle his anger before it took control of him and caused him to do something impulsive and dangerous.

He moved the glasses along the scattered trees and lower hills at the edge of the valley, searching for something to use as a firing position, as a plan was formulating in his mind. Their camp was directly below him, a little over a mile away. They were at the edge of the trees and scattered about between the tree line and the meandering Muddy Creek. The creek had over time carved its way through the valley and high-water during spring runoff had made the creek bed deeper, leaving caving banks of red clay soil that now shielded the horse herd that grazed near the water.

He slowly squinted his eyes, thinking, planning, plotting every move. A glance to the sun showed little time before dusk and he could make his move in the dim light, but he saw the gathering clouds and wispy lace of storm clouds, probably dropping some snow on the high peaks. He was well practiced at stealth, having done it many times for the Berdan Sharpshooters in the early years of the war. He was one of the best for his years with his brothers in the woods stalking game and each other had sharpened his skills beyond the norm even before the advanced training as a sharpshooter. Although he had good cover all the way to their camp, he did not know if he would be able to get to Elly, but he could wreak havoc on the Comanche that would give him an opportunity to free his woman.

He crabbed back from the edge of the flattop, returning to the horses and his gear. He had brought the recently traded-for bow and quiver of arrows, but he wasn't too sure about using them. He strung the bow, nocked an arrow, and let the arrow fly at the chosen target of the heavy headed yellow mountain gumweed. It was at least twenty yards away and the arrow flew true. When Reuben retrieved the arrow, he was pleased to see it was buried in the scrub growth at least a hand width. With a grin, he slipped the bow over his shoulder and hung the quiver from his belt.

A glance to the sun told him light was fading and the Comanche would soon be dousing their fires. But the big silver moon was already showing itself at his back as if promising to light his way. He swung aboard Blue, grabbed the lead for the appy and with a hand signal, motioned to Bear to follow. Pointing Blue to the edge of the flat-top mountain and a dim trail in the trees, he planned on moving closer, using a finger ridge that stretched between him and the camp, and slowly and quietly picked his way through the trees and down the pine needle covered trail to his pre-selected site. He wanted the horses closer, less than a mile or so from the camp but separated from the others so as not to give any whinny or other noise to alarm the Comanche.

He reined up and stepped down, lashed the reins and lead over a branch of a big juniper, and began to ready himself. He looked at Bear, knowing he would stay by his side, but Reuben preferred to go it alone, although any attempt at restraining Bear would only result in a howl-ing, growling dog that would alarm the Comanche. He lightly slapped his leg and Bear came to him, dropping to his haunches and looking up as if asking for orders. "You're gonna hafta mind me boy, we can't be lettin' the Comanche know where we are, so, stay with me and be quiet." He dropped his hand to the big dog's head, rubbed his scruff and slung his Sharps over his shoulder, letting it hang muzzle down from the sling and started to the trees.

The dim light of dusk was a good mask for his movements as he slowly crawled to his first chosen firing point. The wind was at his face, the cool breeze made all the more cool by the mountain storm to the northwest of the camp. A big stack of rocks sat beside a cluster of juniper and cedar, allowing him to ready his position for the Sharps. This was his preferred promontory that afforded him a view of the entire camp and was high enough he could also see into the draw that held the horses. He was a little more than two hundred yards from the camp and with this elevated point, he commanded the entire encampment.

He waited a moment, took another look at the camp, dropped below the crest, and cupped his hands to make the cry of the great horned owl, hoping Elly would hear and know he was near. Without waiting he started moving closer to his second preselected point. The long finger ridge provided ample cover and he was able to quickly move closer at a crouch, but rising to the crest of the ridge, he dropped to his belly and crawled to the top. A scraggly cedar looked like a monstrous skeleton in the shadows of the dim light of fading dusk. The flat boulder beside the cedar offered an excellent view of the camp, even into the tree line, but the shadows were darkening, and the fires had been snuffed. This point was closer to the camp and nearer the tree line.

His plan was to do what he could up close with knife and bow, move away to the Sharps, before making it back to the horses. He lay still, observing the movements of the warriors as they prepared their blankets for the night. The captives were huddled together in the trees, and several of the warriors spread their blankets close to the group, making a human chain or barrier to any that might try to escape. He lay the unstrung bow and quiver under the limbs of the cedar and near the rock and backed away, dropping below the crest of the narrow ridge.

He returned to the higher promontory where he left his Sharps, wanting a better look at the camp and the movement of any Comanche, if there were lookouts, guards, or others that would be a problem. He lay belly down, using the field glasses that were only somewhat helpful, the fading light making it difficult. He found three sentinels, one near the women, one overlooking the horses, although there were three or four others stationed around the horse herd, and one near the trail that brought them from the upper valley and the camps of the Apache and Ute.

Reuben frowned, thinking they were somewhat careless with so few on guard, but after a decisive victory, their confidence in themselves and disdain for their enemy was giving them a sense of complacency. That overconfidence would work in his favor, and he grinned at the thought. He had estimated there were about forty warriors and remembered seeing dust further down the valley that prompted him to surmise that several had continued on their return to their village, leaving the others to bring the captives and the horses. But that also told him their village was not too far away which meant he might not have much opportunity to accomplish his plan.

He lowered the field glasses, replaced them in the case that lay beside the Sharps, and reached out to Bear, running his fingers through his scruff. He whispered, "Well boy, we need to give 'em time to get asleep, sound asleep, before I start this, and I'm gonna need you to be on your best behavior." The dog scooted closer to his man, leaned his head into the petting, and let his tongue loll out and a big slobber drop to the ground. Reuben shook his head, rolled to his back and slipped his hat down over his eyes, and crossed his arms to get a little shut eye before he started his work.

12 / STEALTH

The cold brought Reuben awake, opening his eyes without moving, he lay beside Bear who had apparently scooted close to Reuben in the night, sharing his thick fur and warmth that kept Reuben asleep. But everything was white, Bear included. The mountain storm had moved down into the valley and was dumping a wet fall snow. He slowly rolled to the side, saw about two to three inches of snow had fallen and the moon was hiding behind the storm clouds. There was no wind, the snow was drifting lazily down, and the brilliance of white gave as good if not better sight of everything around, even though everything was white.

He crawled back to the crest and stretched out beside his Sharps that had been sheltered by the slight overhang of the stack of rocks and looked at the camp below. There was no movement, the horse herd was huddled near the close bank for some protection and were hoarding the warmth of one another. He could see no guards or lookouts and assumed they had sought shelter somewhere. He shook his head, unknowing if the snow would be a help or a hindrance, but he had no choice, he must make a try at freeing Elly and maybe some of the others.

He crabbed back from the crest, came to his feet and in a crouch, trotted to where he left the bow. He took another look from the closer firing point, strung the bow behind the cover of the cedar and with the quiver at his side, he went to the trees. The basin of the camp was sheltered by several hillocks and knobs, all with scattered juniper and piñon, but Reuben stayed below the round-tops, with the only place where he would be exposed was the dry wash that carried runoff in the spring. It was only about fifty feet across and he stayed low and back away from the trail that sided the wash.

He trotted behind the next knob and ridge, making his way to the look out that was stationed near the trail from the upper valley. As he drew near, staying low and using the scattered piñons for cover, the bright white of the fresh snowfall provided all the light he needed. A quick glance to the sky told the storm was passing and the moon was clawing its way from behind the clouds. Reuben nodded, grinning, and stayed immobile watching for the lookout.

Movement near the trail showed the man, stomping his feet and hugging himself, trying to keep the cold at bay. As Reuben expected, the man was more concerned with his own condition in the cold than about any possible adversaries, thinking even the Apache and Ute would have enough sense to wait for the passing of the storm to try anything. As the man turned his back to the trees to look at the trail, Reuben slipped closer, needing to be about forty feet for a killing shot with the bow.

———

FINISHED WITH COOKING THE STRIPS OF VENISON OVER THE small fire, Elly palmed a handful of strips and with head bowed, started to the trees where the other captives were held. Tosahwi, or White Knife, had been her captor and had stood beside her while she tended the meat and put the timpsila in the coals, and now watched as she started to the trees to join the others. He grunted as she walked away, turning to the other warriors beside the fires. He nodded to Isatai, the medicine man, "She is good medicine," and waited for a response from the elder. Isatai, his buffalo horn headdress cocked to the side, grunted, "Her hair is like the meadowlark, but I think her spirit is like *Pia Mupitsi*, the great owl that eats people. Did you not hear the cry of the owl after we stopped?"

"What is unusual about hearing an owl? They are all about us!" declared a frustrated Tosahwi. He shook his head and started away from the fire, but Isatai counseled, "You should seek the guidance of Manitou. To take a woman that is not of our people but of the white eyes, could offend Manitou and bring a curse upon you and your lodge."

Tosahwi stopped and turned back to face the medicine man, "She is a prize of war! No one took such a woman! Manitou has honored me with such a prize!" His words were shouted, a great disrespect of the vaunted medicine man, but Tosahwi was only concerned about himself and his plans for this new woman with hair like the sun. He believed she was a great prize and would bring him many honors and the other warriors would envy him. It was a common practice for warriors to bring captives into their lodges either as wives or to be a slave for their wives. It was a show of strength and was only done by great warriors. He was a great warrior! He shook his head as he stomped toward the women.

He watched as the white woman went among the others, joining herself to two women, one older, and the younger looked like a Mexican, not an Apache. He nodded, remembering these were the women that were in the white man's cabin with the yellow haired one. He was certain it was the older woman that had fired on him and his warriors when they charged the cabin, killing two of his men. She was a warrior, that one. They could not find the rifle when they stormed the cabin, but they took all the women, even though they all fought like wildcats, kicking, and clawing and screaming. He chuckled at the thought, knowing he had captured a woman of spirit and that was good.

Tosahwi turned away and started for the horses. He decided he would take the woman and go, perhaps to the village, perhaps somewhere for just the two of them. He knew of a good place in the foothills where the spirits had carved great temples and caves. It would be a good place to tame his wildcat before taking her to the village.

He rode his mount back to the camp, leading one of the captive horses, a palomino gelding whose hair was like the woman. As he rode to the women, Little Owl stopped him, "What do you do? Were you not told to help bring the captives and horses back to the village?"

"I will take my prize and go off alone for a while. You and the others can do the bidding of Piarʉ Ekarʉhkapʉ, our war leader. But I must do as I would. She is a wildcat that needs to be tamed before I take her to the village."

It was the belief of the Comanche people, as it was with many of native people, that each one is responsible for his own decisions, and it is not right for one to compel another to go against his will. Even the commands of a chief or war leader are not enforced against the will of each man, except in a time of war,

76

then the war leader must be obeyed, but once the battle is over, then each must go his own way. When Tosahwi said it is something he must do, it was not subject to another. Little Owl stepped back, letting Tosahwi ride closer to the women.

As he neared the huddled women, he stepped down and pushed his way through the group, searching for the yellow haired white woman and easily spotted her, sitting with the others from her cabin. He stepped near them, reached for her arm, and jerked her to her feet. Elly fought back, jerking her arm away from him and stepping just out of reach. She glared at the man, spoke in Spanish, "*No me toques!* Don't touch me!" she spat.

Tosahwi grinned, grabbed her arm in an iron grip and turned toward the horses, dragging her behind, shouting and fighting. As they neared the horses, he stopped, drew her close and jerked a long strip of rawhide from his belt and quickly wrapped it around her wrists, and lifted her to the back of the palomino. But the binding had a long line and he swung aboard his blaze faced bay horse and held the binding tight, together with the lead rope of the horse. "If you try anything, I will jerk you off the horse onto your face and drag you behind!" he snarled. With a quick kick of his heels, he started toward the trail, and she grabbed a handful of mane to keep her seat.

Even though dusk had already dimmed its fading light, Tosahwi knew there was a full moon and he planned to go as far as possible toward the place of the caves, even though it was too far to make it in one night. He wanted to be apart from the others so he could have his way with his captive, his first step in taming the wildcat.

Elly was watching the terrain as best she could in the

fading light, even though the full moon hung off their left shoulder, she wanted to know where they were, where they were going, and remember any landmarks that would guide her back home. Some way, whether Reuben could find her or not, she was going to get free from this man and go home to her man. She had been surprised that none of the captors had found the knife she carried in a sling at her back. She had sewn the sling into the lining of her tunic and the knife hung between her shoulder blades, easily concealed from all but a thorough search. Hopefully, she would get a chance to get to it and use it to free herself, but she would have to bide her time, for she had already seen that this man was an experienced warrior and was much stronger; but somehow, someway, she would get free.

13 / AMBUSH

Using the scraggly piñon to shield him, Reuben had moved within range of a bowshot. Bringing the bow to a full draw, he aimed a little high, knowing the dampness in the air could influence the flight of the arrow, and released the shaft. It whispered to its target, taking the lookout in the neck, and stifling any outcry. The Comanche grabbed at his neck as his knees buckled dropping him to his face. A kick and a stifled groan and he lay still. Reuben looked around, moved quickly to the downed warrior, grabbed the collar of his tunic, and dragged him to the back side of the big juniper, relieved him of his weapons and slapped at the branches to drop loose snow on the still form.

A quick glance to the sky told Reuben the snow was lessening, and the moon hung high with a wide halo around it, magnifying the light on the blanket of white. He trotted back to the trees and began his slow stalk toward the lone guard by the women. Although there were several warriors in their blankets around the huddled women, none were within reach, and all were asleep and separated by about five or six feet. Reuben used the shadows of the trees to mask his approach, thankful for the fresh snow that also muffled any sound of his movements.

He spotted the figure of the lone guard, sitting underneath the outspread branches of one of the few ponderosas. As Reuben watched, plotting his approach, the guard's head bobbed, and finally rested on his chest. Keeping his approach from directly behind the ponderosa, Reuben stayed in the shadows, each step calculated and purposeful. He stayed in a crouch, believing he could move faster and even quieter than in a crawl, this was the time of late-night, early morning, when sleep held its tightest grip on the tired warriors and others.

It was but a short while until he neared the ponderosa and slipped his Bowie from the sheath at his belt. Holding it blade up, he made one more step, closer, ready to reach around, when the warrior snorted and jerked himself awake. A deep breath and stretched out arms could be heard and seen from behind, as Reuben stayed as still as the heaviest laden tree, blending with the shadow of the big ponderosa. He waited, saw the man stretch out his legs again and begin to relax. The lookout's breath was ragged, and Reuben waited until it was regular and shallow. The tree was too big to reach around both sides and he dropped to one knee, his left shoulder against the tree, took a deep breath and in an instant, slapped his left hand across the man's mouth as he brought the razor-sharp Bowie blade across his throat, cutting through almost to the spine. The lookout kicked, choked, tried to cry out as he grabbed at his throat. His head dropped and Reuben grabbed at the man's tunic to hold him tight to the tree, steadying the body until it was still and looked like the man was asleep.

It wouldn't be until there was enough light that anyone would see the massive blood sign.

He looked up to see two of the women watching, but none of the sleeping warriors had stirred. He took the guard's knife, hawk, and fusil rifle with the horn and pouch and set them aside. He looked carefully at the sleeping warriors, glanced at the women and one woman motioned toward the guard on the upper edge of the circle. Reuben nodded in return, made a quick glance at the group of women searching for Elly, but did not see her blonde hair. He thought maybe she was sleeping among several of the women that had huddled close for warmth, then he turned his attention to the warrior on the upper edge of the circle.

He moved back into the shadows of the trees, slipped silently around to the upper end of the circle, and slowly peered around a juniper to look at the warrior nearest the women. He lay on his side, facing the women, and he was obviously a big man, and Reuben made a closer look and saw he also had a woman held tight against him, using her for warmth and keeping her to himself. His breathing was regular and raspy, and Reuben began his approach. Within moments he was behind the man and quickly dropped his left hand across the man's mouth as he drove the knife deep in his back, twisting and driving it side to side to destroy the heart. The man struggled, kicked, and bit at Reuben's hand, but the knife did its work and the man's struggles lessened and he lay still.

The woman had rolled away and stared wide-eyed as she watched the struggle, glancing around at the others to see if any of the other warriors were coming awake, but none moved. Reuben looked at the woman to see she was the Mexican girl they had traded from the Apache. She smiled as she recognized Reuben and started to speak, but Reuben put his finger to his mouth to silence the girl. He looked at the others and motioned her to come into the trees with him. As he started away, two of the other women came with the girl and each one carefully and quietly moved to Reuben's side once they were in the shadows.

He was surprised to see the one known as Goos-Cha-Da, and he frowned, looking past them and then to the girl, he whispered, "Where is my woman?"

"The man known as Tosahwi took her! They left right after sundown. They went that way," she pointed to the trail that went further into the cut between the mountains.

"Was she alright?" he asked, squint eyed and angry, not just with the Comanche but with himself for sleeping when they left.

"She was, but that man is a mean one," answered Goos-Cha-Da. "You must get to her soon!"

Reuben looked at the older woman, knowing what she was implying, and he nodded with a glance to the other women. He shook his head and spoke quietly to them, "There are weapons by the tree where the guard sat, and the big man that held you also has some. You women get those and try to help the others, it might be best just to try to slip away, but I will be up on the mountain and when there is more light, I will start shootin'. That would be the best time to make your escape, unless you are found earlier."

The women nodded, and Estrella asked, "Should I go back to the cabin to wait for you?"

"Yes, that would be best." He looked at Goos-Cha-Da. "Will you help her?"

"Yes. I also believe the men of our village will be here

at first light. Your shooting could help them when they attack."

"Well, I'm not waitin' on them. I just want to keep them from comin' after me and the man that took Elly." He nodded and disappeared into the trees. As he trotted around the back side of the small hillocks, he looked to the sky and knew the sun would soon show its face, but he need not wait for the full sun-up to make his attack. Within moments he was back at his promontory, and he began readying his position for his assault. He had mentally plotted two other spots he would move to, firing from each one to make the Comanche believe there were more shooters.

He was just over two hundred yards from the furthest edge of the camp. Most of the warriors had moved their blankets to the edge of the trees in anticipation of the snow, but they were starting to stir. He was surprised there was no alarm about the dead men, but perhaps the women had covered the bodies or something. When several warriors had gathered by the first fire that flared, they stood, hands outstretched to the blaze, when a cry from the trees told Reuben they had found at least one of the dead. He brought his sights to bear on the biggest of those at the fire and had readied his shot, when the cry of alarm sounded, but the target was slow to move, and Reuben dropped the hammer. The big Sharps roared, spat smoke and lead, and before the bullet found its mark, Reuben was on the move.

Many times, he had to reload on the run when he was with the Sharpshooters and that experience proved its worth now. He hurried to his second firing point, dropped to one knee behind the rocks, searched the camp for another target and saw two huddled by the trees, frantically searching the nearby hills for the shooter. But Reuben was much further away than they expected, for never before had they been attacked and shot at by anyone that was more than a hundred yards away.

Reuben steadied his sight, squeezed off his shot, and immediately dropped the lever to open the breech and start reloading. He was on the move to the site beyond the first, and he trotted toward the point, keeping the crest of the ridge between him and the camp. He dropped to his belly in the cold snow, getting a waist full of cold, but he looked at the camp and saw several warriors on the run toward the hills below him. He picked out the leader, followed him as he came nearer, then dropped the hammer again. He watched at the big .52 caliber bullet shattered the man's solar plexus and spat out the back, spraying bright blood on the white snow. The target fell to his back, kicked once, and lay still. The others that had been running beside him, stopped, dropping into the snow, looking for the shooter, shouting to one another.

Again, Reuben was on the move, shoving the paper cartridge into the breech and closing the breech with the lever. He was thumbing the cap on the nipple as he dropped behind the cedar and rocks. He slowly lifted up to see what the warriors were doing, but it appeared they had retreated to the trees. The slow rising sun sent shafts of light through the trees, and Reuben found another target. As he sighted in on the man, he saw others around him and his target appeared to be giving orders to the others, and Reuben nodded, grinning. This was the leader. He narrowed his sight, set the triggers, and slowly squeezed off his shot. It was about two hundred twenty yards, and the bullet quickly found its mark. The man's head exploded before the others, splattering detritus on the group, startling and frightening them, prompting them to move further into the trees.

Reuben grinned and slipped back from his promontory. He dropped below the crest and started back to the horses. Bear had been at his side through the entire attack and stayed with him as he went to the horses. Reuben replaced the reloaded Sharps in the scabbard, hung the bow on the horn of the saddle that was on the appy, then swung aboard Blue. With a hand signal to Bear, they started toward the trail, well downstream and out of sight from the camp.

He had no sooner hit the trail than he heard the sounds of battle from the encampment of the Comanche. He grinned, knowing the Apache, and probably the Ute, had made their move against the raiders, and he knew they would wreak vengeance upon all the Comanche. That was the way of the people, one tribe attacks their enemy, steals horses, takes captives, and that tribe will seek vengeance. For is not that the way of all people? The endless cycle of wars the world over?

14 / SEARCH

The storm chased Tosahwi and Elly from the camp and whistled on their tail as they took to the trail that sided Muddy Creek. As the clouds began to crowd the full moon, Tosahwi turned away from the trail to cross the shallow creek, the horses caved in the edges of the creek bank, before splashing through the icy water and climbing the far bank, breaking away the grassy edge to climb from the arroyo. Tosahwi glanced over his shoulder and up at the sky to see the dark clouds and the wispy skirt of snow, "That will cover our trail! No one will follow!" he declared, nodding to the storm.

Elly glanced back, jerking on the reins of the palomino to make him stumble and dig at the bank, making it cave in and leaving sign for Reuben. Tosahwi jerked at the lead, giving the gold mare leverage with the taut lead as she clawed her way up the bank. Elly had handfuls of mane as she leaned over the withers of the mare, talking to her, and encouraging the mare. "We can make it, girl, keep your head up!" she softly spoke into the mare's ear. She looked back at the trail, hoping to see some sign of Reuben in pursuit, but the growing darkness and the cold wind obscured her view and there was no one. As they left the creek bed, they angled across a flat that flanked several low finger ridges that came from the higher hills.

As they pushed through a cut of a higher ridge, the zig zag of the trail blocked the wind and the brief respite allowed Elly to lie on the mare's neck and draw warmth from the animal. After moving through the cut between the long flat-top ridges, Tosahwi continued to angle to the south, keeping the ridges off their right shoulder and running from the storm. Elly continually looked at the storm clouds, fearful the snow would prevent any pursuer of seeing their tracks and quickly muttered a prayer, "God, please keep the snow away, Reuben must see the tracks. I know he'll be coming. Help him, Lord!" she pleaded, shaking her head, and hugging the horse's neck for any warmth.

They were traveling through a sage brush flat, shadows of hills showing off their right shoulder, when Tosahwi turned into the mouth of a wide draw between smaller timber covered hills. The break from the wind was a relief, when Tosahwi turned toward the timber, taking a narrow trail between the trees, and climbing a slight slope, then stopping before the gaping maw of a cave. The mouth was about fifty feet wide, and the solid rock overhang showed signs of previous camps with black smudges from campfires. Tosahwi dropped to the ground, keeping his grip on the leads and tethers of the mare and Elly.

He growled at her, "Get down! This is where we will stay!"

Elly looked at the black maw of the cave, shook her head and swung her leg over the rump of the mare and belly slid to the ground. Standing beside the mare,

Tosahwi came close and with a tight grip on Elly's arm, he led her into the big opening. As they neared, the dim moonlight showed the sign of previous campfires, a loose stack of wood to the left edge of the opening, and what appeared as a black hole in the back, probably the entrance to the deeper portion of the cave. A chill ran up her back, not from the cold, but from fear of what might happen. She vowed to herself, she would die rather than yield to this man, but how could she escape?

"Make a fire, there!" he demanded, pointing to the nearest fire ring.

"I can't with these!" she chided, holding out her wrists with the rawhide bindings.

Tosahwi glared at her, looked back at the approaching storm, and feeling the cold blast of air whistling through the trees, he turned and slipped his knife from its scabbard and cut her ties. Elly rubbed her wrists as Tosahwi turned to the horses, taking them to the far side of the shelter and tethering them to a scraggly piñon that had a tenuous hold in the rocky wall at the edge of the opening. He knew there was a small grassy basin below the cave where he would let the horses graze, once the storm passed, but for now, they had to be tethered.

Elly went to the stack of wood, gathering an armload and a handful of twigs for kindling and returned to the firepit. She arranged some of the wood, the kindling on the near side of the stack, and looked to Tosahwi. "Do you have lucifers or flint and steel?" The man nodded, reached into a pouch at his waist and brought out a flint and steel, fished in the pouch again and gave her a small reed for tinder.

She bent to the wood, placed the tinder at the edge of the kindling, and struck the flint with the striker steel.

Sparks flew and after a few tries, the tinder began to smoke. She bent low, blowing lightly on the tinder until a small flame sprang to life, then carefully moved the tinder under the kindling, again blowing lightly until the kindling caught. As hungry flames began to lick at the kindling, she brought the larger sticks closer and soon the fire was going. Both stood near, holding hands out to absorb the warmth until Tosahwi went to the small stack of gear and brought out a chunk of meat wrapped in a small hide and handed it to Elly. "Cook!" he demanded, nodding to the flames.

She accepted the bundle, unwrapped the meat and looked at Tosahwi. "Give me a knife to cut it!" and held out her hand. He glared at her, shook his head, and grabbed the bundle back, stepped toward the back where a flat rock sat and began to cut strips from the chunk. He returned, slapped the sliced meat in her hand and turned away. She looked at his back, shook her head and looked at the rocks near the fire. A quick glance to the edge of the mouth of the cave showed some willows and she started toward them until he shouted at her, "NO!" and brought his knife out, brandishing it before him.

She looked at him, shook her head, pointed to the willows, and said, "You get willows so I can cook the meat!"

He glared at her, shook his head, and stomped past her to cut some willow withes. He did not see Elly grinning at his back, as she lifted the corner of her lips and snarled at the man, thinking about how she was going to make his life miserable.

———

89

THE FIRST LIGHT OF EARLY MORNING SHOWED THE patchwork of fresh snow. The wind down the valley had blown most of the snow into drifts in the trees, rocks, and crevices. Yet Reuben knew that even though most of the snow had been blown free from the flats where only bunch grass and cacti would collect the wind-blown snow, it could still obscure any sign of the renegade called Tosahwi who had Elly as his captive. Bear trotted alongside Blue, the appy trailing behind, and when he left the trail beside Reuben, the man reined up and watched as the big dog went to a caved in bank of the creek. Reuben nudged Blue closer, and it was easy to see that two horses had crossed the creek and the caved in bank showed snow filled tracks. He grinned and said to Bear, "Good find, boy, keep it up and we'll find her pretty soon."

With the fresh snow, cool breeze and because Elly was riding a strange horse, Reuben did not expect the dog to track her down, but he was a smart dog and knew what Reuben was looking for and he trotted along the trail, keeping to the tracks, before the others, leading the way. It soon became evident the Comanche captor was not trying to hide his tracks, probably assuming no one would come after him and his captive, and it was to Reuben's advantage for the sign was fresh and deep in the damp ground. He lifted his eyes to the flat-top ridges before him, the rising sun, bathing the timbered slopes in muted shades of gold. The sun was warm on his back and Reuben, having paid little attention to the temperature before this, relished the warmth and flexed his shoulder muscles under the buckskin tunic.

They made the zigzag cut between the flat-top ridges and came into the open and the sage brush flats. With the thick growing sage, greasewood, and cacti, the single trail was the only way to move unhindered. Bear led the way, about thirty yards in the lead and trotting at a steady pace, tongue lolling and tail wagging. As they neared the mouth of a wide draw that nestled between two timbered hills, Reuben whistled the dog back and dropped to the ground beside him. He rubbed the big dog behind the ears and spoke softly to him, "You need to stay close now boy, I'm thinkin' we might find 'em somewhere near. Let's you an' me take it easy now. I'm gonna take the horses to the trees, then we'll go a ways on foot, just in case."

The dog dropped to his haunches until Reuben walked the horses ahead, and he followed close behind. At the end of the rocky point, Reuben tethered the animals, and with his Henry in hand, binoculars in the case at his shoulder, he motioned Bear to climb the slope to the sharp ridge above for he planned to go to the crest and use his field glasses to survey the basin before them.

Bear struggled to work his way between the rocks that formed a rim below the sharp crest of the hill. Reuben slung the Henry at his back and used his hands to climb the steep rocky chute. Once atop the rocks, Bear looked back to Reuben until the man motioned to the top of the hill and the dog began picking his steps through the scrub piñon, rocks, and oak brush. The peak of the hill was littered with massive boulders, as if the Creator had dropped a handful just for decoration. Reuben crouched between two, dug out the binoculars and began his scan. With Bear lying beside him, he took his time as the sun chased shadows away and began to melt the remains of the snow. In the high country, it was common for light snows to be melted away by midday of the next sunny day, and it was rapidly disappearing. Reuben scanned the bottom of the draw, looking for any trail that might have been used by the fleeing warrior and Elly. The draw was no more than a quarter of a mile long where it had a dog-leg bend to the south and a small dead-end basin surrounded by a rimrock edged flat-top mesa on the north, and steep walled rocky slopes on the west and south.

He brought the glasses closer to scan the slopes below him and saw a small grassy basin directly below his promontory atop the rocky hill. He moved to another stack of rocks to get a closer look at the mouth of the draw and the trail up the dry wash. It was there he spotted the trail of the two horses, but it only went around the shoulder of this hill, then bent toward the small basin below. He searched the scattered juniper and piñon, but could see nothing, until he smelled woodsmoke. The thin wisp of smoke rose from between a line of gnarly cedar, and as he focused in on the source, Reuben could tell it was from an overhang and possibly a cave. "Gotcha!" he whispered, prompting Bear to turn quickly to look at his man.

15 / CONFRONTATION

E lly jammed the butt ends of the willows into the dirt beside the fire, letting the thin strips of meat hang over the flames, absorbing the smoke and heat. She stepped back to watch the meat, asked Tosahwi, "Do you have anything else, potatoes, timpsila, or?" she stood with hands out, palms up as she shrugged.

"Meat is good for now!" he declared. "The snow has covered everything. Tomorrow you will find other things."

"Find? We don't find, we trade for them at the traders! I am not your squaw to dig in the dirt for you!" she spat.

Tosahwi reached for her, but she snatched her arm back as she stepped out of his reach, snarling at him like a wild cat. He laughed, "You will do as I tell you or you will not eat! A good beating and you will obey!"

"Ha! You are not man enough to beat me to make me obey you!"

He lunged for her, but she easily stepped back and away from him. She had watched his eyes and knew when his anger would take control for him to make a move. She had been avoiding and outsmarting boys and men most of her life. She had always been a beautiful girl and woman, and the men were attracted to her, but few knew anything about gaining the trust of a woman, until Reuben had rescued her and the other girls from the Cheyenne Dog Soldiers. She had been instantly attracted to him, a man that would risk his life against overwhelming odds to rescue someone he did not know marked him as a man to be trusted and honored. Their mutual attraction was instant and had never waned, and in her spirit, she knew he would come after her and she even believed he was near already.

Tosahwi glared at her, glanced to the meat and his hunger made him choose the meat for now, but he looked at her through squinted eyes and was determined to make her submit to his demands. He snatched at the sizzling meat, tossed it from hand to hand to let it cool, then began gnawing on the hot juicy strips as he glared at the woman.

Elly was on the far side of the fire from Tosahwi and picked her own meat, stick and all, from the flames. She never took her eyes off the man and refused to relax, even for a moment. She knew he wanted her to yield to his demands, but if she could make him think it might be possible, if he were to be patient and less forceful, perhaps it would allow enough time for Reuben to find them.

She dropped her eyes to the meat and in a calm voice, asked, "Do you have other wives?"

"I had a wife and a son, but they died from the white man's spotted disease!" he growled, his anger flaring and revealing much about himself as he chewed on the meat, juices dripping from his chin.

"And you have no woman now?"

"My lodge is empty! Even my wife's mother and sister were taken by the disease!" he spat.

"How long ago?" asked Elly, feigning concern.

"One year ago in the time of colors. White traders brought blankets and capotes that carried the disease, but our people did not know about the spotted sickness. Many of our people died." Tosahwi dropped his eyes to the fire, stared into the hungry flames and remembered. He sat still for some time, his emotions showing in his eyes and countenance. Elly had watched him, keeping her eyes from the flames knowing to look into the fire ruined your night vision and she was thinking about the deeper darkness at the back of the cave, wondering if that might be her escape.

Tosahwi looked up at Elly, "The white man took my woman and child, so I take a woman from the white man!" he declared, nodding toward her and grinning. "You will learn the ways of the Numunuu and be a good wife to me, or you will walk with your ancestors!"

Elly lifted the corner of her lip in a snarl, ."If you try to make me do anything I do not want to do, perhaps you will walk with your ancestors!"

Tosahwi laughed, reaching for another strip of meat, as Elly snatched up the willow withe like a whip and cut it across his eyes, the withe as flexible and cutting as braided rawhide, making him scream and fall back, grabbing at his eyes and kicking out at nothing. Elly grabbed two more willows with meat, a long stick the same size as her arm that had the end in the flames and slammed several hot coals towards Tosahwi, landing on and burning his legs and breechcloth as more ashes and coals bounced at his face. Tosahwi rolled to his side, swatting at the coals, and rubbing his face and eyes, jumped to his feet but stepped on the hot coals and danced like grasshopper on a hot rock. Elly jumped to her feet, turned to the back of the cave, and ran into the blackness as far as she dared, hugging the wall, and squinting her eyes to take advantage of the light from the fire and coals behind her. Her night vision helped, but the blackness was thick and cold.

She stopped, keeping the firebrand before her, shielded from Tosahwi by her body, and searched the darkness. She took several tentative steps, feeling with her toes, knowing that many caverns also held deep chasms and holes that could swallow an unwary person. She whispered a quick prayer, "Lord, you are the light of the world and I need your light now, please guide my steps."

She paused, listening, and heard the drip of water into a pool and knew she had to be careful with every step. The dim light of the firebrand, coals that barely glowed, reflected off shiny surfaces and she squinted, searching, and saw stalagmites and stalactites, wet with seeping ground water. The water flowed into a small stream, no more than a hand's width, that crossed the floor and bent towards the back of the cavern. She looked back to the cave entrance, heard the whimpering and mumbling of the injured Tosahwi, but he was not near, probably trying to clear his eyes of the ashes or the injury inflicted by her whipping the willow across his face.

She shook her head, thinking of her next move, but she was stymied, for there was no air movement, no light showing, but of course it was still dark outside, and maybe, hopefully, there would be some light come the dawn. Her eyes had grown accustomed to the darkness, and she felt her way along the wall, searching for any dry place that would provide some safety. Yet, she knew

Tosahwi was not the kind of man that would give up and allow her to escape. He might know this cave and the deeper cavern and know there was no escape. All he would have to do is wait her out or make a torch with a sap-laden pine branch and come searching for her. But if he did, she would be ready for him. She reached behind her neck to touch the butt of her knife that hung from the sling, just for reassurance.

———

A QUICK GLANCE TO THE SUN SHOWED IT WAS STILL MID-morning and the sun was warm on his back, but Reuben was thinking only of Elly, wanting to know what was happening in the cave below and if she was safe. He looked below, saw movement and Bear came to his feet, a low growl coming from deep in his chest. Reuben put his hand on his scruff. "Easy boy, don't give us away," as he watched Tosahwi lead two horses from the overhang. The warrior picketed the horses on long rawhide leads and started back to the cave. Bear's muscles tensed, eager to take off after the man, somehow knowing this man had something to do with Elly. "Not yet," whispered Reuben, watching the man disappear below the overhang.

He gave him a few moments, then crabbed back from the edge, motioning Bear to stay at his side, and the two worked their way back toward the horses. When they came to the rimrock, Reuben led the way down the long chute, sliding on his feet and rump, Bear coming close behind. He went to check on the horses, loosened their girths and led them off the point to a patch of grass and picketed them on a long lead. He replaced the binocular case behind his cantle, slipped the Sharps into the scabbard and withdrew the Henry from the scabbard on the other side. He jacked a round into the chamber, swapped his possibles bag with the accouterments for the Sharps for two handfuls of cartridges for the Henry. Tucked a second loaded cylinder for the Remington pistol into the loop at his belt and motioned for Bear to join him.

He stayed in the trees, even though the sun and wind had yet to dispose of the fresh snow, but he wanted to make his approach to the cave silently. As he flanked the hill, a slight trail through the trees took him toward the small basin where the Comanche had picketed his horses before the mouth of the cave. As he neared the overhang, Reuben slowed, watching for any movement, and carefully and quietly made his approach, moving from juniper to piñon, staying in the shadows and avoiding outlining himself against the remaining snow.

The mouth of the cave was in the shadows, no light showed from a fire, but a thin tendril of smoke twisted through a split in the overhang and sought the blue sky with skeletal fingers. Reuben peered through the thin branches of the scraggly piñon, his shallow breathing slowly allowing his chest to lift and fall, the only movement of the man in the shadows. As he watched, searching, Tosahwi stood behind the dwindling coals, pushing more sticks into the coals and stretching, wiped at his leggings and breechcloth. He stepped closer to the edge of the overhang, the morning sun searching the dark entrance, and showed himself. His face was streaked with black over the yellow and red that had been his war paint. Reuben watched as the man lifted a waterbag and poured it over his face, even into his eyes, then bend over, shaking his head and long hair as he lowered the bag and replaced the stopper. He held a rag in his hand and wiped at his face, taking special care around his eyes, then wiping most of the war paint and black streaks from his face.

Reuben frowned, looking behind the man and searching the cave opening, hoping for some movement or something that told of Elly's presence. Her absence bothered him, his imagination thinking the worst, and he gritted his teeth, working the muscles in his cheeks, trying to stifle his anger. Bear let a low growl come, but Reuben's touch stifled the beast's protest. Reuben took a deep breath, lifted the Henry before his chest and stepped away from the piñon. "TOSAHWI!" he shouted, moving quickly into the open at the edge of the small basin meadow.

He stood boldly before the Comanche, saw the man stand unmoving before him and watched as he rubbed at his eyes. Reuben shouted, "You stole my woman! I am here to face this Comanch!" he spat the words and continued. "Will you hide in your hole like the prairie dog you are, or will you come and face me?! I will cut your hide from you while you scream like whistle pigs of the desert! My woman will take your meat and beat it with the chokecherries and bitter juniper berries and feed it to rattlesnakes and the field mice, but even they will spit you out!"

He paused, watching the man who still rubbed at his eyes. Something was wrong, why did he not respond, and where was Elly?

Tosahwi stood tall, pushing out his bone breastplate covered chest, flung his arms out wide and shouted back, "Who is this prairie chicken that squawks before my camp? Why do you whine before me before you die? You stink like the striped back skunk that waddles through the woods and you dare to talk to me?"

"I am Reuben! The man that tamed the wildcat you

took from the cabin by the Jicarilla Apache! I am
surprised to find you alive! She probably saved you for
me! Or did she already take your manhood and feed it to
you? Is that why you stumbled around? Did she already
make you into a woman?"

"Aiiieeee!" screamed Tosahwi as he strode boldly
from the mouth of the cave. He held only a knife, his
other arm outstretched as he moved into a crouch and
came closer. Reuben said, "Well, alright then!" and
moved to one side to lean his Henry against a big boulder, place his pistol atop it, and drop his coat beside the
pistol. He watched every step made by Tosahwi, and
continued to face him, drawing his big Bowie knife from
the scabbard at his back and drop into a crouch. The
combatants circled one another, slowly moving their
weapons side to side, watching the eyes of their oppo-
nent, both knowing this would probably be a fight to the
death.

16 / FIGHT

Tosahwi lunged toward Reuben, thinking of ending this fight quickly, but he was surprised when the white man slipped past him, untouched. The warrior spun around, wide-eyed and snarling, and he saw the laughing expression on the man before him. All the times before, Tosahwi's reputation as the best knife fighter among his people had done much to set the tone of the fight with his opponents fearful of what he might do, but this man grinned and even laughed as he easily moved away from Tosahwi's knife.

Tosahwi feinted then swung his knife in a wide sweeping motion, thinking to open the man's belly, but when Reuben tip-toed and sucked in his gut, the only thing besides air that was caught by the knife of the Comanche warrior was a tuft of the buckskin that hung over the man's belt. Reuben danced back and laughed again. "What's the matter, Tosahwi, I thought you were a great warrior?" Reuben moved his Bowie knife, blade up, from hand to hand as he watched the warrior and side stepped around the circle made by their movements.

Tosahwi's eyes flared, and he lunged forward,

sweeping his knife toward Reuben's stomach, but the white man spun around and swept his knife across Tosahwi's back from his left shoulder to his right hip, laying open the buckskin tunic and cutting deep across his back. Blood quickly flowed as the Comanche arched his back and moved away, reaching behind him with his free hand and brought it back bloody.

Tosahwi crouched low, glaring at Reuben, and slowly moved toward him, watching the man's eyes and movements. But Reuben had always waited for the warrior to make the attack and still he waited. Tosahwi quickly feinted, swooping up a handful of dirt with his free hand and throwing it at Reuben's face. The dirt blinded Reuben as he rubbed at his face with his forearm and moved away, but Tosahwi pressed his advantage and thrust the knife at the man's belly, plunging it through the buckskin and into his midriff.

Reuben grunted as he fell and stumbled away from his attacker, giving a back handed swing with his Bowie to keep the man away. He shook his head and wiped at his eyes just as Tosahwi charged again and Reuben sidestepped the charge, bringing his big Bowie down like an axe across the man's shoulder and upper arm, slicing it open and driving the man to his knees. Reuben stepped back, clawing at his eyes, but still watching the warrior, now on his knees and holding his upper arm. Blood flowed over his fingers and knife, yet Tosahwi came to his feet and turned to face Reuben, whose tunic was now bloody and dripping on his leggings.

Tosahwi grinned. "You are bleeding, white man! I have killed you!"

Reuben chuckled. "This?" touching his side with his free hand. "I have had worse than this many times, but your back is split wide open, and you can only use one arm, I think it is you that is done!"

Tosahwi dropped into his crouch, growling, "No white man can kill a Comanche!" He stretched high, arched his back, and shouted to the mountains, "I AM TOSAHWI of the *Yaparʉhka* COMANCHE!" and charged at Reuben.

The sudden lunge surprised Reuben, he thought the man was wounded beyond such a move, but the desperation of Tosahwi drove him. Reuben back pedaled quickly, but a stone rolled under his right foot, causing him to stumble backwards. The driving pain stabbed at his middle and he fell, his arms outstretched to catch himself, but Tosahwi charged, screaming his war cry, and brandishing the knife, blood covering his left arm and death filling his eyes. He saw the man stumble before him and knew this was his last chance to kill the man before him. When Reuben hit the ground, the impact drove the breath from him and he gasped for air, the searing pain in his side feeling like a red-hot poker and he grabbed at his side. Tosahwi was only a step away and Reuben struggled to roll away, but a black cloud seemed to drop between him and the savage Tosahwi.

The growl was like the roar of an avalanche and came from the black mass of fur that showed a gaping mouth full of teeth as it lunged for the Comanche. Tosahwi tried to stop his charge but crashed into the big black beast and Bear's teeth sunk deep in the man's face and neck, the great weight driving the warrior to his back. Tosahwi tried to scream as he frantically fought against the monster, but Bear's grip clenched tighter and ripped a fist sized chunk from the man's neck, blood spurting against his chest. Bear was astraddle the dead warrior and snarled at the remains of his face, but the dog knew the man was dead and with a last threatening growl and a snap of his jaw, Bear turned away and trotted to Reuben.

Reuben sat up, reached for Bear as he came near, and hugged the big dog tightly, caring little for the blood on his scruff and face, grateful for the timely attack. "Bear, boy am I glad you came when you did. I'm afraid I'd be a mite bloodier if you hadn't!" A wet and bloody tongue slobbered all over the side of Reuben's face, but the man did not resist. He struggled to stand and added, "Now, we need to find Elly." He motioned to the cave, "Go! Go find Elly, Boy!"

Bear took off at a run, leaping into the dark maw of the cave and barked as he ran, crying out for the woman of their family. The barks echoed back from the cavern, and Reuben looked at the remaining coals of the fire, found a large stick and stuck the sap laden bark end into the coals, fanning them with his hands. He turned toward the dark hole at the back of the cave, heard the dog whining, but it wasn't the sound of pain but of pleasure. He stared into the darkness, took a few steps, and saw the big dog leading Elly into the open. She smiled. "Well, it took you long enough!" she declared, laughing as they ran to one another.

The embrace was long, but quickly interfered with by Bear, who wanted his share of attention, and the two separated to allow Elly to drop to her knees beside him and give him a big hug. She pulled away when she felt the wet on her face, reached to wipe it away and saw it was blood. She frowned as she looked at Bear, saw no open wounds and asked Reuben, "Has he been hurt?"

"Uh, no. That's not his blood."

She frowned as she stood and cocked her head to the side as she looked at her man, the dark splotch at his side and his hand held to the mass told her he was wounded. She moved quickly beside him, "Is it your blood?" she asked, looking from Reuben to Bear and back.

"Nope," answered Reuben, nodding to the clearing before the cave.

Elly frowned at him and said, "You sit down, I'll tend to that!" and stepped to the opening to look beyond the cave. The mauled body of Tosahwi lay in the trampled down grass, unmoving. She turned back to Reuben, frowning. "I did not hear any gunfire!"

"It took both of us," answered Reuben, nodding to Bear who now lay at his side, panting.

"Then I guess you can give me the details while I bandage that," nodding to his side. She grabbed up Tosahwi's water bag and the parfleche and started to Reuben.

———

THEY KEPT TO THE SOUTH SIDE OF MUDDY CREEK, shielded from view by the cottonwoods, alders, and rampant willows. The half-moon clearing on the north side was split by the meandering dry wash, the only life showing was the gathering of turkey buzzards, ravens, coyotes and more. The carrion eaters were having a feast on the bodies of both horses and warriors of the Comanche. When Reuben did a stealthy scout, he motioned for Elly to bring the horses and join him. They had brought the two horses taken by Tosahwi, and Elly now led Blue with the blaze faced Bay on a lead behind him, while she was astride her familiar Appaloosa and led the palomino.

Reuben swung aboard Blue and started across the killing fields. Buzzards took flight at their approach, but quickly resumed their feast after they passed. Coyotes tucked tail at the sight of the people and the big dog, but a low-slung badger yielded no ground. As they moved among the dead, they saw none that were recognizable and knew the Ute and the Apache had done their work, taking their own dead, if any, with them. As they rode to the small clearing where the captive women had huddled, they were relieved to see no sign of any of the women or children, and after a deep breath of relief, Elly said, "Let's go home!"

AS THEY NEARED THEIR TIMBER COVERED HILLS, THE SUN was cradled by the peaks off their left shoulder, the fading light making the remaining gold of the aspen groves even more predominant. The deep orange and shade of gold of the sunset made the hills and valley come alive with a glow of color and they rode past the Apache camp, saw a lot of activity, but were anxious for their own home and pointed the horses to the saddle crossing and trail to the cabin. As they rode into the clearing before the cabin, they were surprised to see both Estrella and Goos-Cha-Da standing on the porch watching them approach.

Bear beat them to the women, bounding up the steps to greet them like the family members they had become and both women dropped to their knees to give the big dog a hug. Estrella stood as Elly came up the steps and embraced her warmly. Estrella greeted her as she said, "He," nodding to Reuben, "told me to wait for you. I was afraid you would not come. I am glad you did!" she declared and hugged Elly again.

Reuben grinned at the women and stepped down to

begin stripping the horses of their gear. Elly turned to him, "They have supper waiting for us!" she announced, smiling as she hugged both women.

"I'll be right in, this'll only take a minute or so," answered Reuben.

Once the horses were stripped, he led them down the slope to the wide meadow, pushed open the brush gate and let them pass through. He watched as each one rolled, stood tossing their heads, and trotted to the water. The mule and recently acquired palomino trotted to the newcomers, sniffing, and snorting as they sorted out their ranks. Reuben grinned and started back to the cabin, anxious for a good meal. It would also be good to sleep in the cabin tonight. Tomorrow would be soon enough to work on the last of the preparations for winter.

R euben sat on his familiar promontory, watching
the shadows lengthen with the rising of the
sun. He lifted his binoculars for his early morning
scan of the countryside, shrugging his shoulders to
enjoy the growing warmth. The mountains of the
Sangres were shedding the gold and oranges of the
quakies, the scrub oak brush with its dark red was
holding tight to the tiny leaves that colored the lower
skirts of the timber covered mountains. The arching
sky was donning its blue capote, shrugging off any
remains of night clouds. The eastern sky had snuffed
the last of the night lanterns and welcomed the rising
sun that slowly pushed away the blushing colors of
sunrise.

Reuben looked down at the dozing dog at his side,
the big black beast that looked more like a big wolf than
a dog, except for his two patches of white atop his head
and chest. He lightly stroked the animal's head, "Well
boy, I ain't too sure we wanna go back to the cabin. The
women said they'd be workin' them hides most of the
day, and that's messy business. I know they won't put

you to work, but I'm not too sure about me. Maybe we oughta go do a little huntin', ya' reckon?"

Bear lifted his head and bent around to look at the man beside him, leaned his head against the man's leg allowing him to stroke his fur, and dropped his chin between his paws and closed his eyes to resume his snooze. Reuben chuckled. "You're no help!"

But Reuben's stomach reminded him he had yet to have breakfast, so the man decided to return to the cabin, just as soon as he finished his scan of the territory. With the sun now bending golden lances across the hill-tops and into the valley, he lifted the binoculars for a more intense search of their lands. Yet the search revealed nothing alarming, a herd of elk was moving into the grassy flats to the west of the creek, a few pronghorn antelope were getting their morning drink, and about a dozen deer were grazing on the last of the green grass this side of the willow shrouded creek.

He dropped the glasses and sat back to enjoy the first warmth of early morning, enjoying the line of sunlight slowly crawling down the mountains, giving first light to the dusting of snow on the mountain peaks. It was already unusually warm for this time of year. The high mountain country, although having already shed the first snowfall, was feeling more like late summer than early winter. He leaned forward, elbows on knees and remembered how his father had called this time the second summer, or the rare warm times after the first frost, Indian summer. His father had explained he thought the name came from the practice of some native people who would burn off the last of their harvest just prior to winter, causing a smoky haze to fill the land and what seemed like unusual warmth. "Whatever the reason, it's one of my favorite times," declared his father, slapping his hand on Reuben's knee, "I just wish it'd come ever' year!"

Reuben smiled at the memory of his father and their times on the farm in Michigan territory during his youth. It was there he and his brothers honed their skills at stalking animals, and sometimes one another, and their marksmanship with their rifles. Ammunition was in short supply, and they had to make every shot count, a practice that had shaped his abilities with his rifle.

With the sun showing its golden knob over the eastern hills, Reuben rose, rifle in hand, binoculars in the case, Bible under his arm and Bear at his side, to return to the cabin and enjoy some breakfast. As they moved from the trees to the saddle crossing, he glanced toward the camp of the Jicarilla, and they appeared to be busier than usual. He paused as he watched a moment before realizing they were packing up to move. He knew the Ute would travel their oft used trail that crossed the Arkansas and took them to the hills above Colorado City and the land of many hot springs, which was their usual winter encampment, but he did not know where the Apache would travel to for their cold weather abode. *Maybe Goos-Cha-Da would know if she's still here.*

He was pleased to see the women busy with the hides, as they had been for most of the previous week. Elly had been anxious to learn the way of brain-tanning and had traded with Goos for the lessons. She admitted it was hard work, "But it's so rewarding, to see the finished pelts that can be made into coats and more!" she exclaimed, though tired, she was still enthusiastic.

She had recruited Reuben to find the many aspen saplings they used to make the hide stretching hoops, the big smooth cottonwood log for scraping, a bundle of lodgepole pine they used for both frames and poles as long handles for the elk scapula they used for stretching and scraping. Just getting the tools to help was tiring and time consuming, but she was learning a skill that would be with her for most of her life and that would benefit the family, and more. He smiled at the thought of family and shook his head as he turned back to the trail to the cabin.

Walking into the clearing before the cabin, he paused and watched the women as Goos began removing the stretched hides from the hoop frames. They had applied the brain slurry the previous afternoon and Elly and Estrella were now busy at the last stretching and final scraping, using the stretched hides to support them as they crawled across the hides, using the scapula scrapers to clean off any last tidbits. Elly looked up and smiled. "Your breakfast is waiting by the fire. There's some cornmeal biscuits, meat, and gravy. The coffee's also ready. I'd join you, but..." and shrugged as she motioned to the hides, "we need to ready them for smoking. There's much to do, as you can see."

Reuben smiled, "Me'n Bear will make do!" and motioned the big dog to the porch. He took the steps in two long strides, mounted the porch, and looked back at the littered yard. They had six wolf pelts, all prepared with the hair on, and would soon put them over the smoke and finish the job. Elly had already said she planned to make winter coats for them both with the pelts, but that would be later. He turned into the cabin and went to the fireplace for his breakfast, dished up some biscuits, added some meat and covered it with gravy, poured a big cup of coffee and went back out on the porch to eat and watch the women. Bear stayed at his side and plopped down beside the bench, dropping his head between his paws.

"It looks like your people were packin' up to leave, Goos. Are they goin' to their winter camp?" asked Reuben, as he sipped on his coffee.

Goos looked up to the porch, nodding, "Yes, they are going."

He noticed she said 'they' and wondered until Elly said, "I've asked Goos to stay the winter with us, but we've also talked about taking Estrella back to her family."

The women were working well together, as Goos started shaping a large frame to hang the hides over the smoke from the fire that was yet to be built, but as soon as Elly and Estrella finished, they joined Goos who began giving the directions for Elly and Estrella to begin tying the hides over the framework of saplings that were bent into the rough shape of a small wickiup, or dome. Reuben watched as they worked, wondering about the overlay of the hides, but was confident Goos was well-experienced and knew what must be done. He thought about what Elly had said, frowning, thinking that all he knew about Estrella was that she had been taken from her family by a raid of young bucks from the Llaneros Apache. But where her home was, he was not certain.

"So, when were you thinkin' about makin' this trip for Estrella?" he called out from the porch, finishing up his biscuits and sitting back.

"Oh, after we're done here. Goos said it's only about three, four days ride, that way," nodding to the Sangre de Cristo range.

Reuben frowned, "That way?" he asked, standing to look at the mountains with the dusting of snow above timberline. "You mean, over those mountains!?"

"Ummhmm, that's right," she answered, smiling as she fussed with a particularly large pelt.

"Uh, haven't you noticed, it's wintertime up there!" he responded, pointing to the long range of towering granite tipped peaks.

"Oh, we'll have time. Goos said so!" said Elly, smiling.

Reuben shook his head, mumbling to himself, *Oh, I suppose she has some kinda control over the weather, huh?* he thought, as the idea of crossing the high mountains made him shiver as he looked in the distance. "How long's it take to smoke 'em?" asked Reuben, leaning against the porch post, coffee in hand, as he nodded to the dome smoke house.

Goos responded, "They will be finished by this time tomorrow." She was crawling toward the fire rings, a basket load of wood chips and twigs in hand, readying to start the fires. It would take some tending to get a good start, but the wet chips and green limbs would turn the hot coals into a smoke fountain that would require constant tending through the night and following day.

Reuben looked to the mountains again, saw the clear, blue sky arching overhead, felt the warmth of the sun and thought, *Sounds like we'll be spending the rest of this Indian Summer on the trail. Sure hope it lasts!*

The sun was at their back as they rode past the site of the Apache encampment. Little sign showed anyone had been there, much less an entire village for some time. Reuben mused as he remembered the many campsites he had visited between Michigan territory and the Colorado territory Rocky Mountains, most left by pilgrims and prospectors, but almost all left with refuse and trash that told of the disregard and total lack of concern of people that thought no one would ever know they had passed through. The land was so vast and empty, perhaps they thought that no harm would come of their left behind rubbish, but to Reuben, it showed a contempt for the Creator who fashioned this land for the use but also the stewardship of its inhabitants. As he considered the thoughts, he knew it was the natives' way to respect the land and all that it held, for it was from the land they gained their life and livelihood.

They angled southwesterly across the valley, crossing the shallow and rippling creek that wound its way through the valley that lay in the shadows of the sawtooth Sangre de Cristo mountains. Known as Grape

Creek, the twisting and winding stream was constantly gathering willows, alders, chokecherries and more as a cloak to shelter the crystal-clear waters teeming with trout. On the trail for most of the day, they were aiming for the black timbered skirt on the flanks of the mountains that showed a split in its hem that marked the trail told of by Goos-Cha-Da, the woman of the Llaneros band of the Jicarilla Apache, who had bonded herself to Elly as a teacher in the ways of the people. She said, "This is the way my people go to return to the land of their winter village. There are many wickiups and old people that stayed behind. On this return journey, they will take more game before returning to the village and prepare for the time of cold days."

The sign of the passing band was plentiful, with many horses, travois, and people walking, the trail was wide, and undergrowth trampled down. It was late afternoon when they came upon the site of the village's camp from the night before. "They've made good time, seein' as how not all of 'em are mounted and they're draggin' them travois," observed Reuben, looking around at what had been the campsite of the villagers. Again, little sign was left apart from the obvious grazed over grasses and the well-traveled trail, made even more so by the dragged travois and the numbers of travelers.

Goos-Cha-Da had reined her mount around to ride along the edge of the camp, staying near the scattered aspen and pines that marked the flank of the ridges. Reuben watched, frowning, as she swung down and examined something on the ground, touching the dirt and looking ahead. *She's trackin' somethin',* he thought. Goos looked to her friends, swung back aboard the palomino, and nudged the mare closer to the others. "They are being followed," nodding toward where she had checked the sign. "There are four riders, Comanche, following."

"How can you tell they're Comanche?" asked Reuben.

"Their moccasins. The Comanche make the bottoms," lifting her foot and crossing her leg over the withers of the mare to show the bottom of her moccasin, "of buffalo hide, stitching it here," pointing to the edge of the moccasin, lower than where hers were stitched. "When they kneel or push away, the stitching shows, and the thicker leather of the soles leave a different track."

Reuben glanced at a grinning Elly who wore an expression as she looked at her man that said, "I told you!" but she did not speak. Reuben just shook his head and looked back at Goos. "What do you think four warriors would do, that's a whole village and they have many warriors. Surely they have someone watchin' their back trail."

"They do, but the Comanche are just scouting. They stay too far behind."

"Scouting? Why?"

Goos twisted around, pointing along the lower tree line, "There is where the Comanche took us after the fight at our village, and there is where many of their warriors died. You killed many. It is the way of the people to seek vengeance on their enemies. When one tribe suffers great loss, their warriors want to kill as many or more of their enemy."

"Does it ever end?" asked Reuben, knowing the way of the natives was not so different than other people the world over. It was what was happening in the east and south of the country, where men in grey were fighting men in blue, many were friends, neighbors, and even brothers until the war broke out. Now, when the north wins a battle, the south want revenge, and so it goes, continuing until many die solely for the never-ending cycle of revenge. Were they so different than the natives, or was it just the evil in man that is never satisfied?

Reuben looked at Goos. "Do you think we should warn your people?"

"They will know, but the Comanche will not come this way to attack our people. Beyond there," pointing to the timbered shoulders of the high peaks, "or where our winter encampment lies. My people know this and will prepare. Even now, they are moving to better places to fight."

"Will those scouts come back this way, or stay on the trail of your people?"

"They will return to their people and tell of what they have seen. Their trail follows that of our village, but they will only go over the crest to see where my people will go, then the scouts will return to tell their war leaders."

Reuben glanced to the sun that was lowering above the long line of peaks, and to the trail that moved into the trees"Maybe we should make camp for the night, get an early start in the mornin'. I don't want to get caught out in the open by those scouts."

With only a nod to one another, the three women slipped from their mounts and began preparing the fire for the meal. Reuben tended the horses, stripping the gear, letting them roll, and taking them to water. With a pack horse and a pack mule, Blue and the appaloosa, and two palominos, he was busy with the bunch. Bear drifted over to the women, expecting some scraps to eat, but bellied down and dropped his chin between his paws to watch the women cut meat, vegetables, and prepare the corn meal biscuits to bake in the Dutch oven.

Reuben stood back to judge the lay of the campsite, picking the best places for the sleeping blankets, but also approaches for any attackers. The hair at the back of his neck was telling him there was something amiss and he was determined to make this a safe camp, but also prepare for what he expected from the Comanche. Even if the scouts had followed the villagers, if they returned, they would easily find the sign of their passing and with as many horses as they had, it would be a tempting prize, especially if they scouted it out and found there were three women and only one man. He breathed deep and searched for a high promontory that he could glass the area roundabout, and maybe get a better perspective of their camp and any vulnerable points.

With the scope mounted on the Sharps, the binoculars in the case at his side, he pushed his way through the trees, searching for a trail that would take him to the rocky escarpment that shouldered out from the trees just below the ridgetop and overlooked their camp and the trail going further up the mountain. Their camp was just up from the confluence of two mountain streams that formed what was well known as Muddy Creek and lay in the shadows of the black timber that climbed the flanks of the ridge. Goos had directed them to follow the same trail made by the Apache that angled to the southwest from the promontory divide that split the runoff streams to flow north and south. Once across the divide, the trail crossed the rolling hills toward the long timbered finger ridge that marked the south end of the valley and pointed west to the towering peaks and Medano pass.

A quick glance to the west and the towering mountains showed the peaks had ducked their heads into the clouds that could be storm clouds, but the lowering sun was painting them in shades of gold and orange, casting the golden glow on the valley below. Reuben's chosen promontory was the knobby end of a line of rimrock that hung just below the crest of the finger ridge, but the bulbous end afforded good cover and was high enough to see over the ridge, as well as several miles west and up the valley. Although the valley made a wide dog leg bend, the willow lined creek twisted its way around the point and forced the creek side trail nearer the ridge, making it easier to see.

He stood beside the weathered dead skeleton of a cedar tree, using its shape to mask his own, and with it as support, lifted his glasses for a long survey of the trail and valley above and below their camp. About a mile above their camp, a small herd of elk had taken water and were lazily grazing on the grasses between the creek and the tree line on the south edge of the creek. Reuben counted four cows, three gangly legged yearling calves, and two small bulls, the smaller one having long spike antlers, the larger showing about five points on each side. The larger bull stretched out his neck and appeared to grunt at the others, pushing them to the trees where Reuben saw a bit of a trail that followed the contour of the ridge up and over. He watched as the bull pushed his small harem up the trail, over the ridge and start across the narrower dry gulch on the far side. They had no sooner entered the gulch, than the cows spooked and took to the timber, the bull chasing after them.

Reuben dropped the glasses, stared at the scene, then lifted the glasses again to see four riders coming down the draw, two by two, and obviously warriors. Their attire told him they were the Comanche scouts spoken of by Goos. He twisted around, following the draw with his glasses to the lower end and saw where that draw joined with the wider green valley that carried the creek. *If they go to the end, they'll probably pick up our sign and come to investigate.* He twisted back around, made another quick scan of both the green valley and the dry gulch, and turned to get a better look at the terrain around their camp. Another glance to the sky told there would be at least another hour or more of light, the dusk offering enough vision to make a fight. They might be defending it soon, and he wanted to know every place of cover and more.

I tehtah'o, Burnt Meat, was the leader of the band of four Comanche scouts and the only proven warrior of the four. It was customary for a warrior to take young, unproven, men on a scout to give them experience before they are sent into battle, but often the scouts would result in conflict or even battle. Itehtah'o was considered a good leader and one that would soon become a leader of raids and perhaps become a war leader. He had been answering many questions from the young men, but they had grown silent as they were returning to the village to report their scout on the Apache that were returning to their winter encampment.

The setting sun was strutting its last display of colors, stretching their shadows long before them, when Itehtah'o nudged his mount to the left and across the tracks of the many Apache that passed through the days before. Buffalo Horn, Dog Eater, and Loud Talker frowned as they watched their leader, but were quick to rein up and watch to see what had concerned him. Itehtah'o slipped to the ground and examined the tracks that joined those of the Jicarilla. He looked back to the northeast, then turned to look up the grassy draw that carried the south fork of Muddy Creek. With another closer examination of the tracks, Itehtah'o stood and swung back aboard his mount and motioned the others to join him.

As they neared, the leader pointed to the tracks and asked, "Buffalo Horn, Dog Eater, when did those horses pass here?"

The two men slipped to the ground and looked closely at the tracks, then looked up the draw. Horn answered, "Before the sun touched the mountains!"

"Dog Eater, how many horses?"

Dog Eater looked at the sign again, turned toward Itehtah'o. "One hand, perhaps one more. Two were led behind others."

The younger men looked expectantly to their leader, hopeful of a possible raid on this small group, probably an Apache family left behind for some reason and now wanting to rejoin their village. The leader looked over the three, turned to Loud Talker. "You, go! Scout but do not be seen. They are in camp now, not far. We will wait here."

The young man known as Loud Talker dug his heels into the ribs of his mount and took off up the draw, but quickly went to the trees to cover his approach. The sun had dropped behind the mountains but still sent long lances of gold and more into the cloudless sky, heralding the end of the day and leaving the last gift of dusk, when Loud Talker returned. With a broad grin, he eagerly reported, "Three women! One with hair like," then glanced around and pointed to the gold lances that speared the sky, "like the sun! Another one is young, Mexican, the other older, Apache. I saw no man."

Upon hearing the report of the yellow haired woman,

Itehtah'o remembered the woman taken by Tosahwi and that Tosahwi had never returned to the village. Perhaps this was the same woman, but how could a woman escape from the great warrior Tosahwi? He let a deep breath escape as he considered the possible prize that was awaiting their taking, then began directing the young men that were eager for honors to be earned in battle and prizes, like the women and horses. They looked at one another, smiles splitting their faces and their eagerness showing as they lifted their lances and bows. Only Itehtah'o had a rifle, but the others had an eagerness that often-outweighed caution.

———

REUBEN STAYED ON HIS PROMONTORY LONG ENOUGH TO see the four scouts cross the trail of the Apache convoy and they appeared to spot the tracks of Reuben and company. He watched as one was sent into the trees, probably to scout out their camp, and Reuben knew an attack would be forthcoming. He took to the trail to return to the camp, moving quickly down the steep slope and coming into the edge of the camp. He called to the women to come to the edge of the trees quickly and as soon as they stood before him, he explained, "The four Comanche scouts are about to mount an attack on our camp. I don't know if they know I'm here or not, but one of them just scouted our camp and returned to the others. Now, here's what we'll do..." and quickly explained his plan for their defense.

Goos and Estrella returned to the fire, intent on tending the food. Goos had Reuben's pistol in her belt at her back, Estrella had Elly's Pocket Colt in her belt. Both women acted as if nothing was wrong, squatted before the fire and chattered among themselves to make every-thing appear normal. Bear had gone with Elly, who was now concealed in the scrub oak at the edge of the ridge, and Reuben was in the trees beyond the camp. Both Elly and Reuben had their Henry rifles and were well concealed.

Leaving their horses tethered in the trees, the four Comanche started toward their assigned points with Itehtah'o, Buffalo Horn, and Loud Talker all going to the far edge of the creek and using the willows and alders as cover to make their approach. Loud Talker was to go the furthest upstream and move across the draw to the tree line above the camp, while Dog Eater made his approach through the trees to move to the camp from the lower end.

Itehtah'o and Buffalo Horn dropped to a knee as the leader motioned Loud Talker to move on to his point. Itehtah'o and Horn peered through the brush, trying to see into the camp, but the fading light showed little more than shadows. The horses were tethered at the back edge of the trees, the cookfire illuminated the faces of the two women, but the long shadows obscured any view of the woman with the yellow hair.

Itehtah'o knew the young men would move quickly to their positions, their excitement making them eager to be the first to take a prize. He saw the shadow of the crouched Loud Talker move into the trees and they waited, giving the man time to move closer to the camp. It was up to Itehtah'o to make the first move, the others to follow, but he waited, wanting the young men to learn patience.

A LOW GROWL FROM BEAR WARNED ELLY AS SHE crouched behind the oak brush at the edge of the trees. She glanced down to the dog to see he was looking into the trees behind her. She slowly turned and watched, trying to see into the shadows, but the trees were somewhat sparse, and the fading light still showed through the patchwork of juniper and piñon and a shadow moved, bringing Bear slowly to his feet. The dog looked at Elly as she moved from the brush into the trees behind the young warrior. She was no more than twenty feet behind the man when she spoke softly, "Détente o muere!" She had spoken in Spanish to say, 'Stop or Die!'

The man turned quickly, eyes wide, but Elly was on his right side, slightly behind him, and he was carrying a bow with an arrow nocked. To bring it to bear, he would have to turn completely around and when he saw her standing with a rifle at her shoulder, he paused. But he could not be taken by a woman and started to turn and bring his bow in line, but Bear would not allow it and lunged from the shadows, his open mouth practically engulfing the man's face as the big dog bore him to the ground. Bear landed astraddle of the struggling man who had dropped his bow and was trying to reach his knife, but Bear shook his head side to side, ripping at the man's throat and tearing his face. Blood spurted, feet were kicking, but within seconds the man's life was taken from him and he lay still.

Although it was a vicious attack and seemed like it should have resounded through the trees, it had been almost completely silent, with nothing more than a slight murmur escaping and nothing loud enough to carry beyond the tree line. Elly dropped to her knees beside Bear, stroking the scruff of his neck and speaking softly to her friend. She glanced at the bloody remains of the young man and stood, turning her back to the sight and focusing her attention on the camp, watching for the others to attack.

———

As Loud Talker stealthily moved through the trees, anxious to get into position before Itehtah'o started the attack, he was focused on his chosen position behind the lone big ponderosa. As many young men, unproven in battle, do, he was too focused on one thing and paid little attention to all else. The shadow that stood beside the spindly snag of the lightning struck spruce was unseen, and the young man moved close beside the skeletal trunk, watching every step but keeping his eyes on the glimmering fire in the camp. Careful with each movement, feeling each step before transferring his weight, it was only a brief glimpse of a shadow that crossed before him before the razor-sharp blade split his throat and neck, warm blood spilling on his chest before he fell on his face. One kick was the only move he made, choking on his own blood that silenced him from muttering his last words.

Reuben went to one knee beside the young man that would never be called a warrior and had died without any prize or honor and wiped the big Bowie knife on the man's leggings, ensured he was dead, and rose to move a little closer to the camp, wanting to see the others make their attack. He was certain the women were in no danger, nor were the horses, for these warriors would want both the women and horses to take back to their people as bounties of war. But he also knew there is nothing guaranteed in battle, and he did not want to risk the women's lives.

ITEHTAH! O GLANCED TO BUFFALO HORN, MOTIONED FOR him to move out and both men rose from the willows, waded across the shallow creek, and pushed through the willows and alders. The creek was about thirty yards from the edge of the camp clearing, and they moved in a low crouch, the grasses muffling any sound of their approach. But the two figures, moving and in the open with the dim light of dusk coming from the mountains, were seen by the women at the fire. Goos whispered to Estrella, "They come," and scooted away from the girl, giving them both room to move about if necessary.

Reuben saw the women move, stepped a little closer and looked down the slight slope and saw shadows in the tall grass, believing it to be the other Comanche. Across the camp and also in the trees, Elly, with Bear at her side, stood in the shadow of the big juniper and watched as the two warriors worked their way closer.

Itehtah'o believed the women, with the fire before them and busy with the work of preparing the meal, would be unable to see them in the tall grasses and dim light of dusk. But the women had been cautioned by Reuben about preserving their night vision, although dusk was hardly the dark of night, but the women had kept a pan or wood always between them and the fire, never looking directly into the flames.

Itehtah'o had told the other young men that he would scream his war cry as a sign for them to attack and with a nod to Buffalo Horn, the two slowly rose and the leader leaned back and screamed his war cry to the tree-tops, and both charged toward the fire at a run. Itehtah'o fired his flintlock at Goos, but the heavy cast iron pot she held deflected the bullet and she rocked back on her heels, reaching for the pistol in her belt. Bear lunged from the trees, his black image appearing as a ghostly shadow, but his growl and open maw startled Itehtah'o who turned to face this phantom of the dark, wide-eyed, and screaming as the big dog bore him to the ground and ripped at his throat. Buffalo Horn was shocked at the sight of the black beast and turned to fire his bow, but Goos had brought the Remington pistol to bear, and the weapon barked from beyond the fire, the bullet taking Horn in the shoulder, making him drop his bow and go to his knees, his hand at his wound, blood pulsing through his fingers.

Reuben walked from the trees, his Henry held at his side, the muzzle toward Buffalo Horn as the man grimaced and rocked on his haunches in pain. Elly came into the circle of light, called Bear to her side, and went to her knees to talk to the champion of the battle. Goos and Estrella stood behind the fire, looking from Elly to Reuben and to the wounded Comanche. Elly asked, "So, what do we do with him?"

"Patch him up, I reckon," offered Reuben, shaking his head. "Or I s'pose we could just let him bleed out, or..." and shrugged his shoulders. He looked at Goos and Estrella and asked, "What do you think?"

Goos was remembering the attack of the Comanche on her village and the time each of the women had spent as captives and made the motion to slit his throat, but Estrella did not speak or move, just glared at the young man. Apparently, he could understand the Spanish they spoke and was fearful of what the women might do, for among his people, the worst thing that could happen to a captive, was to be turned over to the women.

Reuben shook his head, looked to Elly, "You women patch him up. I'll get their horses."

The morning air was cool on their faces, the trail sided the creek that had pushed up against the south edge of the wide draw, hugging the tree line, and the slow rising sun at their backs did little to discourage the cool of the mountain morning. The wide draw ended at a jumble of timber-covered foothills that were crowded together as an assortment of ridges and long hills that fell from the long ridge that paralleled the mountain range. Goos pointed to the ridge and a slight dip that birthed an east west ridge, "That is what is called Medano pass. My people cross the ridge there and follow the arroyo with the creek that is swallowed by the big sand hills."

Reuben frowned, "The creek is swallowed by sand hills?" he looked at Goos, not understanding.

Goos smiled, looked around and pointed to a small anthill of red and black ants. "Like that, only very," stretching her arms high and to the side, "big! Too big to walk across. We will ride around."

Reuben looked at Elly, "This I've gotta see. 'Bout the

time you think you've seen it all, lo and behold, there's somethin' you never expected."

He looked at Goos, "Is the village close by the sand hills?"

She shook her head, "No, no, far to the south across the wide valley."

"How many days?"

"Three, four days."

"How long do you think it'll take that Comanche to walk to his people?" He glanced at the four horses of the Comanche stretched out on leads behind the women. Reuben and Elly trailed the pack horse and mule, the two women led the horses taken from the raiders.

"One day, no more."

"And for his people to find your village and attack?" asked Reuben, frowning.

"The same, perhaps more," she shrugged, knowing many things could determine when the Comanche would leave their village, how many would come and which route they would choose.

"And to take Estrella back to her people?"

"Her people are in a different place. Her people are there," she motioned off her left shoulder and beyond the mountains. "My people are there, beyond the big valley," pointing to the west directly over the mountain range.

Estrella had told them her father had a farm near San Luis and often supplied livestock to Fort Garland to be a part of the annuities promised to the Tabeguache Ute that had agreed to the treaty. San Luis was south of Fort Garland, but the winter encampment of the Jicarilla was a day's ride west of the fort.

He twisted around in his saddle to look back at Estrella, "We'll hafta see where the Comanche might be, we can't let them attack the Apache without warnin'," he said, shrugging. He knew she had mixed emotions about the Apache, for it was an Apache raid that took her from her family and sold her to Reuben and Elly, but she had grown fond of Goos. When Reuben said they would take her home, she could hardly believe it, but now they were on their way, and she did not want to delay her home-going for anything.

She glanced from Reuben to Elly and back to Goos, and with a nod, she answered, "What you think is right, we will do," and forced a smile, but dropped her eyes.

Bear had taken the lead and disappeared into the trees as the trail angled up the side of a knob hill that marked a long round top ridge that pointed to the notch previously pointed out by Goos. The trail they followed wound its way through the spruce and fir trees that topped the long ridge, a few patches of aspen that still stubbornly clung to their golden leaves added contrast to the trek. Once they crested the pass, the black timber failed to yield a view of the valley below, but the trail twisted around a knoll and dropped into the headwaters of the Medano creek. White barked aspen sided the small creek as a clearing less than a hundred yards wide shouldered up against the long line of timber-covered foothills on their left. Reuben nodded to the creek. "Let's give the horses a break, get 'em some water and stretch our legs."

The smiles on the women's faces were contagious and soon the women were moving about, Estrella picking flowers, while Goos pointed out some Buffalo Berries and raspberries for Elly while she dug some Camas roots. Reuben stayed close to the horses that were ground tied, but he was not certain the Comanche ponies were used to ground tying. With nothing more than a loose trailing lead rope, ground tying was used for short stops and horses that were well trained with the practice and could be counted on not to stray. But Reuben knew horses were herd animals and Blue had already established himself as the leader, and the mule had always stayed close by his friend's side, both staying true to their training of cropping grass within reach of their ground tie and no further.

By late mid-morning, they were on the trail that wove in and out of the tree line, riding the flank of the south-facing slopes of the many ridges that stretched like fingers from the granite tipped peak high above their right shoulder. Reuben's glance brought a grin to his face as he thought that mountain appeared to be stretching its hoary head into the clouds. The trail, sometimes steeply dropping away, stood above the lower treetops and the rocky ridges with cliff-like limestone on the north, and sharp-edged steep ridges on the south, both giving way to appear as the hands of the Creator holding the panorama of a wide valley and distant mountains. But the rider's reverie was interrupted when Reuben reined up and held his hand high to stop the others. He stood in his stirrups and sniffed at the air, slowly shaking his head. He glanced at Elly and said, "I'm not sure, but that smells like bear. You smell it?"

Elly shook her head, "I smell something, but maybe its that bunch of elk coming from the trees down below," she suggested as she pointed to the bunch of brown backed and yellow-rumped animals coming from the trees. Reuben turned to look, frowned, and slowly shook his head, "Maybe," he answered and nudged Blue to take the trail at a walk. Bear had been scouting the trail but had fallen back to walk beside Elly and her appaloosa.

Suddenly, Bear trotted up beside Reuben, hackles raised as he growled and dropped his head, his shoulders bunched. "What is it, boy?" asked Reuben, looking at the dog, but the question had barely left his lips when he saw the tree line explode and a massive grizzly lunge after a yearling elk, bowling him over and spooking the others that took flight for the creek and the steep slope beyond. The bear had sunk his teeth in the neck of the young elk, shaking it side to side and breaking the animal's neck. Gangly legs kicked to the side, but the bulk of the bear lay on the carcass and the movement quickly ceased.

Beside the creek, a cow elk stopped and stared at the carnage that used to be her calf. She trembled, standing spread legged, her mother's instinct wanting to protect her calf, but knowing it was too late. The grizzly, now astraddle of the calf, lifted his bloody face to look at the cow, but she turned, jumped the creek, and disappeared after the others.

Even though the grizzly was just shy of three hundred yards downstream from them, the horses had whiffed the beast and were a little skittish. Reuben turned from the trail and into a gulley thick with aspen and that carried a little stream to lead the others about fifty yards into the trees. He found a little clearing and stepped down. "This'll do for noonin'. That way the bear'll prob'ly be gone when we move out and the horses'll be easier to handle. Don't wanna get bucked off and hafta walk out, ya reckon?"

Elly chuckled, "Good choice. Although *I* probably wouldn't get bucked off, I'd hate to have to pick you up!" She laughed as she stepped down and handed the lead line of her mount and the pack horse to Reuben. The other women followed her example and Reuben was soon trying his best to handle all the horses, get them to water, and keep from losing any of them.

The women soon had a small fire going and Goos

B.N. RUNDELL

was cutting the last of the fresh meat into thin strips to hang over the flames. She looked to Elly, "If you'll wash those roots, you can push them into the coals, and we'll have something to go with the meat."

After the meal, Reuben suggested they rest the horses a bit more, give the bear time to leave, and he took to the ridge with his glasses to scan the area. He was relieved to see the bear had wasted no time dragging his kill into the trees and the drag marks told him the bear was on the near side, but the trail crossed the creek and hugged the far shoulders, making their passage through the aspen on the north side safer. When he returned to the camp, the ladies were restless and wanted to be on the way and when he nodded his agreement, the smiles spread all around and they were soon back on the trail.

134

21 / SAWATCH

The sun hung high in the clear blue sky, empty of clouds, the blue arched overhead as a colorful canopy holding only the brilliance of the afternoon sun. The trail between the buttes sided the Medano Creek that meandered through the thickets of willow, alder, and chokecherry. The horses were watchful and somewhat fearful for they could still smell the blood of the grizzly's kill and the stench of the bear hung heavy in the air. The horses were skittish, looking about them and prancing on light hooves that clattered on the hardpacked trail. Within just over a mile, the smells changed to the musky scent of moldy aspen leaves and the freshness of pines. The juniper were thick, and the berries carried a sharp, biting scent, that was somewhat pleasant after the smells of death and more.

Reuben and Elly rode side by side, taking in the approaching view of the distant valley that hung between the mountain slopes shouldering in on either side of the Medano Creek arroyo. The sand dunes were showing as a smooth but rumpled blanket, tossed about from the previous night's use, but stretching several miles before them. The bright sun glistened on the surface of a lake that lay beyond the dunes and contrasted with the dry, dusty, sandhills. Further still rose a stretch of snow-capped mountain peaks that juxtaposed themselves in the far west to frame the masterpiece of God's panorama.

Reuben reined up, looked to Elly, and smiled, "Have you ever seen anythin' with so much contrast and beauty?" nodding toward the wide valley and beyond.

The mouth of the Medano arroyo opened wide to show the expanse of dunes that stretched five miles to the west and lay at a width of over eight miles. The sandhills appeared as waves of water, rippling, and rolling with the overtures of the wind, yet stationary as if frozen in time just for the travelers to see the magnificence and imagination of the Creator. The heat from the midday sun shone in their face, but Reuben shaded his eyes to look at the long lake that lay beyond the dunes. Goos came alongside, "The lake is shallow, mostly alkaline, but there are fish in the deep water." She looked from Reuben to Elly, smiled at the wonder that was painted on their faces, and spoke again, "We will not cross the dunes or the lake, that is called Sawatch Lake. We go there," pointing to the south and a trail that split the flats between the dunes and the timbered flanks of the mountains.

"You have a place in mind for us to camp?" asked Elly.

"Yes, beyond that long mound, there is a creek and small valley with shelter and cover."

"And where is the village of your people?"

"There," stated Goos, pointing to the west beyond the lake and the wide San Luis Valley. "The village is near the El Rio Bravo del Norte, what some call the Rio Grande river."

Reuben had nudged Blue back onto the trail with Bear still running at point. Elly rode beside him and Goos and Estrella close behind. Reuben twisted around in his saddle. "This camp site a good place to get some fresh meat?"

Goos smiled. "Yes, there are deer, elk, and some of the mountain sheep," making a circular motion beside her head to indicate the big horn sheep of the high country.

"Good. I see some deer yonder by the lake, but they're a bit far to try to get without breaking out my Sharps and I didn't want to let everybody in the country know we were hereabouts. I thought I'd take my bow and get something after we make camp."

"Maybe you should gather the firewood and make the cookfire, let me go hunting for a change," suggested Elly, smiling at her man mischievously.

"You've had my cooking and if you all want to eat good, you know I'm not the one to do the cooking!" declared Reuben.

"Are you sure you're the one to do the hunting?" giggled Elly, remembering a not so recent failure of Reuben to bring home any meat from his hunting expedition.

"One time! One time I don't get somethin' and you ain't never gonna forget it!" he shook his head as he grumbled. But both knew it was all in good humor that the remarks were made, for Reuben had more often than not proven himself to be an exceptional hunter.

He glanced at the distant lake, noting the wide alkali seep on one edge, the shallow waters with cattail, and what appeared as a wide wet meadow on this side of the water. Even at this distance he recognized alkali bulrush, pondweed, cattail, and a big patch of bulrush. At the lower end, the deep color showed a depth of water that was not common throughout the rest of the lake, but the wetlands had attracted a variety of wildlife. He turned and looked down the trail, saw the long alluvial fan that had come from the high mountains over many eons and now spread over a mile into the valley and rose over seven hundred feet higher than the valley floor. Holding a cover of sporadic juniper, piñon, cedar and a smattering of ponderosa, the mound seemed to force its way, unbidden, into the flats of the valley.

The trail angled up the slope to cross over and down the far side into the narrow valley of the small creek that wound its way through the gravelly bottom. Goos had taken the lead and brought them to a sizable, grassy, clearing beside the stream where the willows were thin and the water easily accessible. She turned to look at the others, watching Reuben for his acceptance, and with his nod, she slid to the ground to start her duties. Reuben took the horses, stripped the gear, let them roll and picketed them near the water and grass which the animals eagerly began to graze.

With his Henry slung over his back, the quiver of arrows hanging from his belt at his side and the bow in hand, Reuben stepped nearer the makings of the fire and reached around Elly's waist to draw her near and give her a warm embrace. She smiled up at him. "So, is that in case you don't get anything?" she giggled.

"Just never you mind, little girl, you keep talkin' like that you're gonna jinx me and I might not get anythin', and we'll all go hungry!" he answered, smiling but trying to appear stern.

He turned away and walked from the clearing, taking to the trees along the flank of the slope, intent on using the trees for cover to look for any deer coming down to water. A quick glance to the sun showed the distant mountains cradling the golden orb that stretched brilliant lances to herald the last moments of sunlight. He moved silently through the trees, watching the creek bank, and searching for any game trails that might reveal the presence of game. Movement caught his eye and he dropped behind a big ponderosa, nocking an arrow in anticipation.

A lone fawn with scant traces of his spots remaining, gamboled down the trail before his mother, enjoying the liberty of youth. As they neared the tree line, a muted bleat from the mother stopped the fawn in his tracks, bending his head around to look at her and wait for her to move beside him. The doe tiptoed into the clearing, looked about, and with a nod to the youngster, both trotted to the creek side for their evening water. Reuben waited for any others to join them, but within a short while, both mother and fawn returned to the trees, leaving Reuben behind.

He rose from behind the ponderosa and moved further downstream, but there were no other game animals to be seen, nor did he see much sign of recent passage of any deer or elk. Goos had said the villagers had taken the direct route across the flats because they came to the edge of the valley much earlier in the day and had time to make the crossing. Reuben saw no sign of any others that might have used this same area to camp, at least no sign of recent passage. He turned back to retrace his steps and return to the camp, empty handed, and knew Elly would not let him soon forget. But as he neared, he frowned as he caught the scent of meat cooking and wondered just what the women had done.

He stepped into the clearing to see two skewers of

B.N. RUNDELL

birds sizzling over the fire and he looked at the women, all of whom smiled back as Elly asked, "No meat?" and nodded to the skewers. "Goos got us a couple sage hens, don't they look good?"

Reuben shook his head, mumbled something under his breath about women ganging up on him, and walked to the stack of gear to replace the bow and quiver, thinking *At least I won't have to eat crow!*

"But this will be the last time to trade with the Comanche before the winter comes! You have come with us before and we need your woman, she is a good translator!" declared Mateo Cardenas, the leader of the small band of traders from Cimarron, San Luis and other villages to the south. They were commonly called Comancheros because they traded with the Comanche. Licensed by the Commandant of Fort Garland, Colonel John P. Slough Santiago Esquibel had only recently begun trading with the Comanche. Less than two years earlier, his wife, Jimena, was killed during a raid from the Apache and his daughter, Estrella, was taken captive. He had since taken a new wife, a young woman, White Flower, whose father was Comanche and mother had been a captive from a Mexican settlement near Cimarron. She had taken the name of Mayte after she was bought from the Comanche by Santiago Esquibel. Santiago believed by trading with the Comanche and other tribes, he might one day find his daughter and perhaps buy her back from her captors.

"You mean you need me to come, since I have the

license from the Commander of the Fort!" answered Santiago, shaking his head. He stepped away from Mateo, looked at the man's loaded pack mules and back to Mateo. "I have few goods left to trade. I was planning a trip to Santa Fe before starting the trades in the Spring."

"We have much goods, cloth, flour, tobacco, tools, knives, hatchets, and this time, we have rifles and powder! And, if you come with us, you will share in our profits!" offered Mateo. He knew if he was caught trading with any of the plains tribes without a license, the military could take him into the stockade and if he could not pay the penalty, he would be forced to serve his time at hard labor. His license was for the territory of New Mexico and the Llano Estacado, but he was not allowed to trade in Colorado territory on his license, although his scouts had found the Comanche camped in the Huerfano valley east of the Sangre de Cristo mountains.

"Where are you going to meet the Comanche to trade," asked Santiago, considering the offer.

"On the west side of Sangre de Cristo pass, in the valley at the base of the mountains."

It was a common practice for the traders to join with one another to make a trade fair and encourage different tribes to come, demanding peace during the trading time, but recently the Comanche have been less than friendly with other tribes to the west but maintained their peaceful alliance with the Kiowa and Cheyenne.

"Will there be other tribes beside the Comanche?" asked Santiago.

"Ahh, we do not know for sure, but possibly," answered Mateo, glancing to his other partners, Sebastián Ochoa, and Alejandro Fuentes.

"Which band of the Comanche?"

"*Yaparʉhka* Band of the Comanche, those known as Root-eaters, their chief is Piarʉ Ekarʉhkapʉ, or Big Red Meat."

Santiago frowned at Mateo, thinking about the band he spoke of, and knowing he had not traded with them for they were a tribe of the north and east and he had not been in their land as a trader. Mateo saw Santiago was considering and thinking, knowing his purpose of trading was to find his daughter who had been taken by the Apache. "My scout says this band has recently raided the Mouache Ute and the Jicarilla Apache and took many captives."

Santiago looked at Mateo, glanced to the sun and back to the trader. "I will get my things together and packed. We will be ready in one hour!"

Mateo smiled and stretched out his hand to shake. "It will be good to be together again as we trade. It will be profitable for us!" shaking his hand enthusiastically. He turned to his partners, nodding, and motioned for them to take the mules to water and check the loads before they moved out again.

———

"I CAN RIDE, AND I CAN FIGHT!" SPAT BUFFALO HORN as Little Owl of the *Yaparʉhka* Band of the Comanche moved about the warriors, recruiting a raiding party to go against the Llaneros band of the Jicarilla Apache. Owl sneered at the man, "You are wounded and still bleed, you will be a burden to us!"

"No! I must go to get vengeance upon those that killed my brothers on the scout!"

"If you were a good warrior, you would have killed

them or died as you fought against them! Instead, you crawled away like a whipped dog to return to our village and your woman!"

"But only I can show you the ones that killed our warriors! There were two hands of the Apache that attacked us from ambush, and they all had rifles! I demand vengeance!" stated Buffalo Horn, drawing on the conscience of the self-appointed war leader and the way of his people.

Little Owl shook his head but knew he could not deny the man the chance to get vengeance against their enemy. But they would ride hard and far and if he could not keep up, they would leave him behind. As they talked, the cry of alarm came from the edge of the village, causing everyone to grab weapons and turn toward the cry, but they quickly recognized the scout from the Comanchero traders, Candelario Cardenas. He was greeted by the leader of the village, Big Red Meat, who motioned to the elders and other leaders to join him. With a simple nod from the chief to Little Owl, the war leader knew he was to be a part of this council. He glanced at the warriors he had already spoken to, "I will return, prepare yourselves for the raid!" and turned to follow the others into the lodge of the chief.

When the leaders and elders had settled into their places around the central fire, the visitor responded to the nod from the chief and stood, "I come for the traders from Cimarron, Mateo Cardenas and Sebastian Ochoa. We have had many trades with the Comanche of the *Kuhtsutuuka* band, Buffalo-Eaters, the *Kwaaru Nuu*, Antelope-Eaters, and other bands of your people. Since the winds of winter have been stilled, and the cold has not come, it is a good time for one more time of trade with one another. Mateo and Sebastian have gathered many trade goods, including rifles and more, to make a good trade with the *Yaparʉhka*." He paused, looking around the circle to see the response of the leaders to the possibility of trading for the much-coveted rifles. "You have had good hunts and I am told you had a good raid on the Ute and the Apache, now this is a time to make trade."

The men of the circle looked to one another, talking quietly, but unable to hide the enthusiasm at the possibility of gaining rifles and arming their warriors better than ever before. It was because of the rifles in the hands of the Ute and the Apache that their raid had been costly, and they lost many of their young men, but if they could trade for rifles, then perhaps they could gain the vengeance their warriors were demanding.

The chief looked at the others, lifted his eyes to the Comanchero and asked, "Will your traders come to our village?"

"They will meet you at the park at the crest of the Sangre de Cristo pass. As we speak, they are already on their way and should be there in one or two days," explained Candelario.

Little Owl protested, "We are already preparing for a raid on the Apache! Our scouts have told us they are on their way to their winter encampment, and we can attack before they are ready to defend themselves!"

The men of the circle reacted to Little Owl's remarks by slapping the ground before them in protest until the chief lifted his hand for silence and looked at Little Owl. "Would it not be better if your warriors had rifles?"

Little Owl sat back on his haunches, stifling his anger, and slowly nodded. "But we do not know if these rifles are anything but the cast offs of the white man and good for nothing!"

The chief looked to the trader, nodded for his

answer, and the man spoke, "These are new rifles, the same rifles that the white man is using in his war in the east. They are better weapons than any Comanche or Apache has now!"

His remark elicited much response from all the leaders, kindling the look of lust in their eyes and the anticipation of profitable trades unlike any before. Little Owl quickly responded, "Then we must prepare for this trade and if we can go armed with rifles, we will continue to the village of the Apache and bring vengeance upon them!"

War cries filled the lodge of the chief and the leaders and elders came from the lodge, excitement written on their faces as the word quickly spread about the coming trade fair and the possibility of gaining rifles for their warriors. When the word reached Buffalo Horn and the others, the men scattered to their lodges to gather their possible trade goods, hides, pelts, and more, all eager to make a trade that would bring them the sought-after white man's rifles.

23 / SEPARATION

"My people must know the Comanche are following them and will soon attack our village! When they struck our village before, we had no warning and they came upon us suddenly, causing many to cross over to the other side. I cannot let that happen again!" declared Goos-Cha-Da, her fear and frustration showing in her face. She wore a choker of many rows of hair pipe bones interspersed with silver and turquoise beads that bounced with every exclamation. She was seated on the wide grey log beside the fire, staring at Reuben and Elly as they listened to her plea.

Reuben glanced to Elly and back to Goos, "Your people do need to be warned, but we also promised Estrella that we would take her to her home. It was the Apache that raided her village and took her captive, but she must be returned to her people." He paused, looking from Goos to Estrella and to his woman, shook his head and poked at the coals with a long willow stick, then looked back to Goos.

"Could you make it to your village by yourself?"

asked Reuben, although he was hesitant for her to make the long trek alone.

Goos let a slow grin cross her face as she slowly nodded, "You forget that I am Apache!" she declared.

Elly reached over to touch Reuben's knee and looked at her man, "If she took the horses of the Comanche, she could change often and maybe make it to her village before dawn."

Reuben looked at Goos, "Could you? If you had the four horses, switched often, and kept ridin', could you make it by yourself and get there before dawn?"

Goos gave it a quick thought, nodded her head, "I could do that, but I need a weapon."

Reuben grinned, "We took several from the Comanche. There's a rifle, a couple bows and quivers of arrows, and a couple tomahawks. You could take your pick or take all of 'em if you want."

"With that many horses and weapons, in the eyes of my people, I would be a rich woman!" proclaimed Goos, grinning.

Reuben glanced to Elly, stood, and looked at the low-lying moon that showed itself clearly in the fading light of dusk, "Looks like it's gonna be a three-quarter moon, bright enough for a good ride." He looked to Goos, "You gather your gear and weapons together; I'll get the horses."

Elly folded one of the spare blankets to make a pouch for the last of the sage hen meat and the left-over biscuits, tied it across the back of Goos' blanket she used for a makeshift saddle. The Comanche scouts had ridden with nothing more than blankets and a cinch strap with loop stirrups, common among the plains Indians that rode as one with their horses. The spare horses had the extra weapons and other blankets well secured, and the lead ropes had them strung out one behind the other, leads tied to tails, making it easier to lead and keep the animals in a single line behind Goos.

She swung aboard the black gelding, leaned down to grasp Elly's hand and said, "Look for me in the time of green-up. I will come to your cabin, and we can work the hides together."

"I'm counting on that, and I will look forward to seeing you. You have been a good friend, Goos, and I will be praying for you," said Elly, smiling up at her friend.

With a nod to all, she turned the black and started from the camp. The others watched as she rode away into the silvery blue of the moonlight, quickly disappearing into the shadows of the scattered juniper. Once away from the camp, she dug heels into the ribs of the black and set the pace at a canter, careful to keep clear of the greasewood, sage, and cacti, but watching as best she could for any sign of prairie dog villages or rabbit holes. She was anxious to rejoin her people, but aware of the dangers of crossing the flats by moonlight.

Elly leaned against Reuben, looked up at him and asked, "You think she'll be alright?"

Reuben chuckled a little, looking down at the expectant expression of his wife, "She's probably as concerned about us as you are about her! She's headin' home and we're out here in the middle of nowhere with no idea what we're up against."

"I'm not afraid! I've got you to protect me!" smiled Elly, drawing him close.

"But who's gonna protect me?" asked Reuben, his arm encircling his woman.

"Me and Bear!" declared Estrella, kneeling beside the big dog, her arm around his neck, as she looked at her friends, smiling.

"Then we have nothin' to worry about!" answered Reuben. "So, I suggest we get some shut-eye 'fore the sun peeks over those mountains back yonder," nodding to the silhouetted peaks behind them.

As they settled into their blankets, Elly asked, "Goos said Estrella's home, San Luis, is a couple days south, but we go past Fort Garland to get there. Are we going to stop at the Fort?"

Reuben turned on his side to look at his woman in the moonlight that filtered through the branches of the big juniper, smiled, and asked, "Why? Somethin' you need from the Sutler's?"

She smiled at her man, "No, but don't you think they might like to know about the possible fight between the Comanche and Apache?"

Reuben pursed his lips and nodded, "Prob'ly. I think I'd also like to ask 'em if they know anything about the Espinosas, you remember those brothers that killed all those men in South Park."

"Ummhmm, didn't you say one of 'em got away and prob'ly came into this valley, somewhere near the fort?"

"That's what most the men in the posse thought, but I don't know for sure. I do know a telegram went out to most places that had a telegrapher, and that would mean the fort prob'ly got one."

Elly frowned as she looked at Reuben, "And you've been fighting shy of anyplace that had a telegram since we left Fairplay. Is that because you don't want to hear from Holladay or the governor?"

"Ummhmm, I just never thought of myself as a deputy marshal and definitely not married to one!" he chuckled as he rolled to his back, putting his hands behind his head to look through the branches at the star-studded sky.

"Well, we better get some sleep if we're gonna get Estrella home anytime soon!" suggested Elly, pulling the blanket up to her chin and smiling at Reuben.

———

THE EASTERN SKY WAS ABLAZE WITH RED BELLIED CLOUDS lying low over the granite peaks of the Sangre de Cristo range. Reuben twisted around to see the reflective glow on the pinnacles of the mountains, the clouds overhead seemed ready to dump their cargo of molten lava upon him while even the tufts of clouds in the western sky blushed pink as all of creation waited breathlessly for the new day to begin.

Reuben sat on a cold mossy boulder with Bear at his feet as he lifted his voice to his Lord, asking for guidance and protection for the day and blessings on those that were dear to him. He looked to the south where the fort lay out of sight and the flats beyond that held the small community of San Luis. The mountains appeared to tuck themselves into the folds of the terrain as they pushed away from the sagebrush flats of the San Luis Valley. Goos had told him of the Mosca pass that lay behind them, splitting the distance between them and Medano pass they had traveled, and of the Sangre de Cristo pass that came from the gap beyond the three sentinel peaks, the tallest being Mount Blanca, that marked the break in the mountain range. She believed the Comanche would come through the Sangre de Cristo pass to launch their attack on the Apache winter encampment. "But they will probably come in the night to pass the fort," she had suggested.

His plan was to search the trail for any sign of the passing of the Comanche, knowing a war party of any size could not pass without leaving ample sign. As the sun bent its golden lances over the mountains, dancing their way across the flats, Reuben lifted his binoculars from the case at his side and began his usual scan of the territory.

As the light increased and shadows lengthened, Reuben watched several groups of deer and antelope taking water in the wetlands below Sawatch Lake. Two ospreys circled overhead and a lone coyote trotted across the sage flats toward the willow lined stream coming from the lake. He scanned the flanks of the mountains, searching for any movement but saw nothing, and moved his field glasses to the tree line due south of his promontory to see only a solitary dust devil beginning its dance into the dry land.

He lowered the glasses and started to put them away when Bear came to his feet, looking back toward the camp. A low growl came from deep in his chest and he leaned forward, a snarl lifting his lip to show his teeth. Reuben turned and brought the glasses up to look back toward the camp as a flash of tan showed through the thicket of juniper above the camp. He kept his eye on the trees but spoke to Bear, "Go, boy!" The big dog lunged forward, taking the trail to the camp in long strides, growling and snapping as he twisted through the trees. Reuben grabbed up his Henry and followed at a run, uncertain what he had seen, but driven by fear of what he thought might be stalking the women.

Bear bounded into the camp, startling the women. Elly quickly snatched up her Henry and jacked a shell into the chamber, watching Bear stop and take up his attack stance. With head lowered, lips snarling, teeth showing, scruff ruffled, he picked up one paw and carefully stepped forward, growling, and snapping as he moved. Reuben charged into the clearing, rifle across his chest as he looked at the women, saw Elly watching the trees that Bear was focused on, and dropped to one knee beside the black dog. "What is it, boy?" he asked, searching the trees.

Suddenly a macabre scream erupted from the trees and Reuben saw the tawny coat of a mountain lion between the branches of the big juniper that sided the clearing. The puma was stalking the camp, drawn by the smell of food but unafraid of the people. Reuben frowned, knowing Cougars would normally avoid man, yet this one was brazenly stalking them. He spoke softly to Elly, "As soon as he's in the clear and you have a good shot, take it! I'll do the same."

The words were no sooner uttered than the big lion tensed and lunged toward Bear who met the big cat in the air. The lion had forepaws extended, big claws showing, mouth open with teeth ready to sink into his prey, but Bear drove all his weight toward the attacker, mouth wide. Neither Reuben nor Elly could take a shot without hitting their dog and the hesitation gave Bear the chance to clamp his teeth on the lower jaw of the cat, his weight greater than the puma, and both went to the ground, but Bear refused to release the cat, driving him to his back. The big claws of the Cougar digging at the thick coat of Bear, but Reuben ran to the side of the entangled beasts, Henry at the ready, and in an instant, Reuben dropped the hammer, the slug driving into the tawny-brown coat of the cat. The Cougar flinched, digging at Bear with his hind feet, attempting to disembowel his attacker, as they rolled over with the cat on top. Elly, fearful for her friend and pet, had stepped closer and as they rolled, she fired into the neck of the Cougar as Reuben fired again, his bullet striking the cat in the lower chest. The bullets drove the life from the cat and Bear flipped the cat over, straddling the animal, shaking his head side to side to finish it off.

Bear released his grip, looked at the lifeless form, and stumbled off the carcass, falling to his side in the dirt. Elly rushed to him, talking softly to him as she quickly examined his body for wounds. When her hand came back wet with blood, her eyes grew wide with fear and she looked for the wound, finding deep parallel claw marks on his left flank, but nothing else. She looked at Reuben who turned to the packs for her ever-present pouch with her remedies and bandages. He handed it to her as Bear's breathing slowed and he licked at Elly's face. She laughed and let him have his way, and as soon as the big dog seemed to relax, she began her ministrations to patch up her friend.

"Look at this!" declared Reuben as he squatted next to the carcass of the mountain lion. He held up the right front leg and paw to show a mangled leg and deformed paw. "That's a recent injury, just barely healin', but with a leg like that, he wouldn't be too good at stalkin' the usual game animals, and definitely could not outrun a deer to take it down. That's why he was comin' to our camp. Prob'ly smelled the cookin', thought we'd be easy pickins'!"

Elly and Estrella had come near to look at the carcass and Elly pointed out, "Looks like he was in a pretty bad fight, there's more wounds back here," pointing to the right flank of the cat, "but they're too old to tell what they were from."

Reuben looked at the recent wounds, "Maybe a grizzly bear. That's the only thing big enough to win a fight with one o' these catamounts!"

"Well, I don't know about you, but I'm hungry! And those eggs are mighty tempting!" suggested Estrella, turning back to the fire.

"Eggs?" asked Reuben as he stood and looked at Elly.

She smiled, nodding, "Ummhmm, Estrella walked downstream a little, found a backwater with cattails and such and discovered a mallard's nest with four eggs. So, we up and cooked 'em!"

"Then let's up and eat 'em!" declared Reuben.

They were soon back on the trail, heading south with the Sangre de Cristos off their left shoulder, the shadows of the big mountains stretching into the edge of the flats that were abundant with sage, greasewood, and cacti. The yellow blooming rabbit brush that stubbornly clung to their blossoms until the snow took them, proliferated the land, interspersed with the spindly cholla, a few that still held their pink blossoms. The sun was warm on their shoulders and the wide-open spaces of the flats that lay below the mountains, offered ample room for Reuben and Elly to ride side by side. Estrella was leading the palomino that had been ridden by Goos and rode the other yellow horse traded from the Apache. Elly trailed the pack horse and Reuben trailed the pack mule. Bear had taken a liking to the girl and trotted alongside her, limping a little from his wounds, but they were in no hurry, and he was able to keep up.

A glance to the high mountains showed a layer of low-lying clouds obscuring the tops of the peaks, looking like a bridal veil over the face of a blushing bride that sought to hide her best features. With the clouds at timberline, the heavy timber draped over the lower slopes and deep draws looked like a patchwork quilt like gramma used to make out of worn-out woolen britches and coats. Most of the aspen had shed their golden leaves, leaving nothing more than skeletal fingers stretching above white barked trunks. The deep green of the fir and pine bristled in the cool breeze that fell from the higher reaches of the mountains, licking at the exposed flesh of the riders prompting them to turn up collars and hunker down into their coats.

The sun was high when Reuben motioned them into the trees for a midday break. He guessed they had covered about ten miles, but with the up and down crossing of the many gullies and ravines that came from the run-off of the mountains, it could be twice that far in actual miles covered. He had sought to stay near the trees, but the long slopes that stretched from the flanks of the mountains and the many arroyos often made that difficult. He was uncomfortable anytime they were exposed in flatland with little or no cover, but he always searched for any place, a low swale, a cluster of piñon, an unusually tall cluster of sagebrush or greasewood, anything that could provide cover for the small group.

They pushed into the thicker juniper but had seen little or no creeks or signs of springs for water. Always one to carry water bags, Reuben used a pot to hold water as he made certain each horse and the mule had a good drink. The sun was high and hot and with little or no cloud cover, the afternoon travel could be even more challenging and dry. Elly and Estrella gathered the left-overs from breakfast, pork belly and cornmeal biscuits, and they had a pleasant and restful break for both them and the horses.

As Goos had explained, they headed due south as they left the flanks of the Sangre de Cristo mountains and sided the low timber-covered foothills that stretched out toward the fort. The flats were thick with the yellow blossomed rabbit brush and appeared like a yellow and billowy blanket as the breeze from the mountains rippled across the drylands. Reuben kept near the foothills, crossing a wide dry gulch before stretching out on the flats. After crossing three more sandy bottomed draws green showed in the distance. It was a welcome sight for the greenery told of fresh water and they were beginning to wonder if there was any water in this flat land of cholla and prickly pear.

It was late afternoon when they approached a willow lined creek that came from the high country and carved its way down a narrow but green valley to stretch out into the flatland. A short distance further and another creek did much the same, coming from a different stretch of mountains that marked the wide cut that held the mountain passes that crossed over to the east. Reuben looked at Elly, pointed to the long narrow draw that held the second creek, and the low cut between the mountains, "Unless I miss my guess, I'm thinkin' that's what they call the Sangre de Cristo Pass and if so, this was also part of the original Santa Fe trail."

"Then that," nodding to their right, "must be Fort Garland," replied Elly.

"Reckon so," agreed Reuben, looking at a few buildings that sat closer to the near creek. "But that looks like a tradin' post of sorts, and maybe a tavern. Prob'ly caters to the soldiers from the fort. That usually happens whenever there's a bunch of soldiers that come payday are lookin' for somethin' to drink and some entertainment."

"Are we stopping there, or at the fort?" asked Elly, cocking her head to the side and giving Reuben a sidelong glance.

He grinned. "The fort, of course. Anythin' we need, supplies or information, we can get at the sutler's at the fort."

As they crossed the first creek, they came to a well-traveled trail that pointed to the mountains and Reuben stepped down to examine the fresh sign. He went to one knee, touched the tracks and looked in the direction of the trail and sign. "Been some travelers along this way, several horses, looks to be, oh, eight, ten maybe. Near as I can tell the way they're all lined out, it's a pack train of sorts. Several riders, maybe five or six, and most of the pack animals are mules. I'd say they crossed this way 'bout this time yesterday."

"But they're going into the mountains, or over the pass, right?" asked Elly.

"Ummhmm," he replied as he stood, then pointing to the mountain pass, "looks like they're goin' over the pass, headin' east. But if they run into them Comanche, they might not get far."

"Think we need to tell the commander of the fort about the Comanche?"

"Yup!" he answered as he swung back aboard Blue. "Let's see if we can find the right man to be talkin' to and let him know what might be comin' his way."

The fort was an assortment of adobe buildings with sod roofs, built in a rectangle around a central rectangular parade ground, a flagpole standing tall in the middle. With a big barn and corrals set apart and across the main roadway that came from the pass, the buildings were well kept and appeared busy with many men about and busy with a variety of duties. As Reuben and company approached, they were directed to the east side of the fort for the sutler's building. As they drew up front, Reuben stepped down, helped Elly and Estrella down and the three walked into the cool building that sported windows on three sides letting light into the darkened interior.

"Howdy, folks! Welcome to Fort Garland! How might we help you?" asked a jovial man with a drooping moustache, red cheeks, chin, and nose, and a friar's circle of hair around his hairless dome.

"Well, a few supplies, some information, and direction to your commandant's office."

"That's easy 'nuff. The commandant's office is in the same building as his quarters, right over yonder, the bigger building of the bunch along there. It's Colonel John P. Slough, that's the commandant. Now as to the supplies, what can I do ye fer?"

Reuben turned to Elly, "I'm gonna walk over and talk to the colonel. You tell him what we need and be sure to get plenty of ammo for all the weapons."

She smiled, "What we need or what we want?"

Reuben chuckled, "Whatever pleases you suits me just fine."

He was shaking his head and laughing softly as he exited the building, headed for the commandant's office. It was just a short walk and he stepped into the open door, paused to let his eyes adjust to the light and nodded to a young man with unruly red hair, and asked, "Is the colonel in?"

"He is, and may I tell him who wants to know?"

"Tell him, Deputy Marshal Reuben Grundy."

The clerk's eyes flared, as he gave Reuben a quick once-over look, and rose to go to the interior of the office and speak to the colonel. He returned quickly and motioned for Reuben to go on into the office. As he entered, he doffed his hat and stepped through the doorway to see the colonel standing with his back to the door as he looked out the window behind his desk. At the sound of footsteps, he turned and looked at Reuben with a critical expression, "Deputy marshal?"

"That's right, but I'm not here on official business.

But I am privy to some information you might be interested in, however."

"And just what information could you have that I would be interested in?"

"Well," he started as he looked around the office and at a chair in front of the desk, lifted his eyes to the colonel with eyebrows raised as if to ask the question if it was alright to be seated and the colonel nodded. Reuben took the chair and looked up at the colonel who was still standing and holding a pipe with a little curl of smoke rising, and said, "We just came from over the mountains where the Comanche recently attacked the Mouache Ute and Jicarilla Apache."

The colonel harumphed, shook his head as he seated himself and with hands clasped and arms stretched across the desk. "That doesn't concern me. First, it's not the territory I am charged to protect, and if it's Indians against Indians, it is of no interest."

"Well, that's not the full story. We were travelin' with an Apache woman, takin' her back to her people that have come back into the San Luis Valley to their winter encampment that I understand is about a day's ride, maybe two, to the west of here, and we were attacked by some Comanche scouts that had scouted the Apache and were on their way to report back to their people."

"Well, it looks like you survived, so?"

Reuben shook his head, his exasperation beginning to show, "We didn't kill them all, one survived and probably went to tell his people. From what I could determine, they plan on comin' over the pass yonder, and strike the Apache village."

The colonel glared at Reuben, trying to determine if he could believe what was being said, then slowly nodded. "So, you're guessing they will come this way and attack the village?"

Reuben chuckled, dropped his eyes, and shook his head, lifted his eyes to the colonel, "I guess you could say that, but after all, can anybody know for sure what the Comanche will do?"

"I know this, just yesterday there was a pack train of Comancheros that passed through, bound for the top of the Sangre de Cristo Pass, to have a trade fair with the Comanche and maybe some others. Any trader must be licensed by us and keep us posted on any trades he plans. In this case it was Santiago Esquibel and company, and they believe the trades will take several days. So, I don't see how the Comanche will be attacking anybody when they're so busy trading."

Reuben frowned at the mention of the trader's name, then asked, "Do you know this man, Esquibel very well?"

"Well enough, why?"

"Did he have a daughter taken by the Apache a while back?"

The colonel frowned, leaned forward, "Yes, but how would you know that?"

"She is with us. We were on our way to take her back to her family."

The colonel leaned back, "Well, that is good news. Then I suggest you and that girl stay here at the fort until they return. I'm certain Santiago would be very glad to see her. He has been making trades with many different tribes, searching for his daughter."

Reuben grinned and started to rise but was stopped by the raised hand of the colonel. "Also, I believe our telegrapher has been holding a telegram for you from of all people, the governor. That's why it was brought to my attention."

Reuben pursed his lips, shook his head slightly. "What does it say?"

"I do not know. The telegrapher just told me it was from the governor."

"We'll find us a place to camp by the creek and wait for the return of the traders, maybe."

"You're welcome to bed down in one of the officer's quarters, we're understaffed due to the war back east and we've plenty of room," offered the colonel, rising and extending his hand.

"I'll talk to the ladies first, but we just might do that. Thank you, Colonel."

25 / WAIT

R euben dragged the chairs out the front door and
sat them by the wall. Elly and Estrella sat beside
one another as Reuben leaned on the hitch rail, his back
to the parade ground. It was a clear night, the air was
warm, and the stars were beginning to light their
lanterns. The usual bustle of the fort had waned, and few
soldiers were out and about. With the hectic schedule of
the post, their day was from "can see to can't see" and
they were constantly busy. Whenever they found themselves in the fort, the non-coms found lots of make-busy
work, so much so that it was a relief to go on patrol or
other duty that let them tend to their sworn responsi-
bilities.

"Tell me about your father, Estrella," suggested Elly,
enjoying the quiet time together.

Estrella smiled, dropped her eyes at the memory of
her family and began, "Mi Madre and Padre were hard
working people. I was the only child, and I did what I
could to help, but mi Padre said I should just help mi
Madre in the house, and he would tend to the animals

164

and more. Mi Padre was very protective of us and worked hard to make a good life for us."

"Did you have any friends or neighbors?" asked Reuben.

"Before we left Cimarron, yes, but at *San Luis de la Culebra*, there was no one near. We met some people at the church in San Luis, but we did not go often."

"The church?" asked Elly.

"Si, it was built in *La Plaza Medio*, it was a small building, and the Sacerdote was an old man."

"So, what do you and your family believe about the church and religion?" asked Elly.

"I do not know very much, but mi Padre often said for us to get to Heaven we had to do many good things and if we did enough, maybe we could make Heaven. He said it was like the scales we saw in the trading post, if we have more good things on one side than the bad things on the other side, then Saint Peter would let us into Heaven." She paused, dropping her eyes to the ground then looked up to Elly, "Is not that why you," nodding to Elly, "and you," nodding to Reuben, "do the things you do? You know, I have seen you," looking at Elly, "praying in the cabin and when we camp, and I know you go up on the mountains very early in the day and take your Bible and Elly says you pray."

Elly glanced to Reuben and back to Estrella. "No, we don't pray and read the Bible so we can go to Heaven. We already know we will go to Heaven," she watched Estrella frown as she said they knew, "we pray to talk to God, and we read the Bible to learn more about Him and how we should live and more. He is, well, like a very good friend that we talk to and ask for help because we love Him, and we know He loves us."

"But how do you *know* you will go to Heaven? Have you already done enough good to get into Heaven?"

Elly glanced to Reuben and nodded for him to answer. He smiled, nodded, and asked, "Would you like us to tell you and show you how we know and how you can know for sure that you will go to Heaven?"

Estrella smiled, nodded enthusiastically, and scooted to the edge of her seat. Reuben asked Elly, "Could you fetch my Bible from our things?"

"Of course," replied Elly and rose to go into the quarters for the Bible. She returned quickly with both the Bible and a candle in a candlestick and handed them to Reuben. Sitting the candlestick with the lighted candle on the hitchrail, he began leafing through the Scriptures.

He looked up at Estrella and asked, "Did you go to school or learn to read?"

Her shoulders slumped and she quietly said, "No, mi Padre did not believe in school for girls." She lifted her eyes to Reuben and nodded. "But I know that is the Bible, God's word. Mi Madre told me about that, and I saw one at the church!"

"Well, I'm goin' to show you here in God's word where He tells us about goin' to Heaven, and I will read it to you. I want you to know, it's what God says, not just what I say, do you understand that?" questioned Reuben.

"Si, si. I want to know this thing you say."

"Well, the first thing you need to know is told here in Ephesians 2:8-9," he pointed to the page and began reading, *"For by grace are ye saved through faith; and that not of yourselves: it is the gift of God: Not of works, lest any man should boast."*

"Now, we'll come back to this, but what I want you to know is what it says about works, or the things we do. See, if gettin' to Heaven was based on the good that we do, then when we get there, some would *boast* or brag about what they did to get to Heaven. And God doesn't want that, so it's not about what *we* do, but about what *Christ has done for us.*

"Now let me explain a little bit more, there are four things we should understand about what God tells us about gettin' to Heaven. The first is that we're not good enough on our own to get there. See here in Romans 5:12, and 6:23, *Wherefore, as by one man, sin entered into the world,* that's Adam, he's the first man to sin, or do wrong, but there's more. *And death by sin; and so death passed upon all men, for that all have sinned.*

"See, when the Bible says death here, that's not just dyin' and goin' to the grave, that's the final death and Hell forever, the penalty for sin. So, He explains that we are faced with that death, because we all," he pointed to his chest and to Elly and to Estrella, "have sinned. Now it says much the same in Romans 6:23 the first part that says, *For the wages of sin is death.* That's what we get for what we've done." He paused, looked at Estrella and asked, "So, all of us have done wrong in our lives, maybe just disobeyin' our parents, or sayin' bad things, or even somethin' worse, but we've all done bad things and that's what He means when he says we've sinned. But here's the best part, God knows that and gives us His special promise, and that's in the rest of verse 23, *But the gift of God is eternal life,* now that eternal life, is to live forever for all eternity, or to live with God in Heaven. And He says it's a gift! And notice the rest of the verse, that gift is *through Jesus Christ our Lord.*

"So, the first thing we need to understand is that we are sinners. Do you agree with that, Estrella?"

She dropped her eyes and took a deep breath, lifted her face to Reuben and glanced to Elly. "Yes, I am a

167

sinner, I have done some bad things. But mi Padre said if we go to confession and pray and ask forgiveness, God will forgive us, does He not?"

Reuben smiled and said, "Yes, God does forgive us when we ask, but let's understand this," he pointed to the Bible. "The first thing is that we are sinners, and the second thing is that there is a penalty or punishment for that sin. He also says that in chapter 3 and verse 23, *For all have sinned and come short of the glory of God.* To come short of the glory of God means to miss Heaven and that is Hell forever or the death that He mentions. Do you understand that penalty or punishment for sin?"

"I think so, si," nodded Estrella, glancing from Reuben to Elly.

"Good, then the next thing we need to know is that Christ paid that penalty for us! See here in Romans chapter five and verse eight, *But God commendeth,* or showed, *his love toward us, in that while we were yet sinners, Christ died for us."* Reuben paused, and explained, "See Estrella, here we are, sinners facin' the penalty or punishment for our sin which is that terrible death that lasts forever, and God wants us to come to Heaven, but we can't because that penalty has to be paid. So, He sent His son, Jesus, to pay the penalty for us. Just like when we went to the Sutler's, and Elly bought that new dress for you. Because of what she did, you get the dress. And now, because of what Jesus did, you can have eternal life as a gift. Remember verse 23 that said, *but the gift of God is eternal life,* or to live forever, that's in Heaven, *through Jesus Christ our Lord."*

Estrella smiled, then her expression turned to a frown as she looked from Elly to Reuben. "But, how do I get that gift? Do I have to do more works, or good things?"

Reuben let a slow smile paint his face, then answered, "No, but the Bible," touching the pages as he turned them, "tells us how to do that. Here in Romans 10:9-10 and verse 13 *That if thou shalt confess with thy mouth the Lord Jesus and shalt believe in thine heart that God hath raised him from the dead, thou shalt be saved. For with the heart man believeth unto righteousness; and with the mouth confession is made unto salvation. For whosoever shall call upon the name of the Lord, shall be saved.*"

"See Estrella, it's that simple and that easy. God made it that way so anyone and everyone could understand and do what He says. See, to *confess with thy mouth* is to pray and to *believe in thine heart* is more than just believin' that he existed. Many people, even the devil, believes that, that's what we call believin' here," tapping his head, "but God says we must believe here," touching his chest for his heart, "that what God says is true and that He sent His son to pay the price for your sin and mine. When we sincerely believe that He says that is *unto salvation* and that when we call upon Him in prayer, believin' that, we *shall be saved.* That means we'll be saved from that second death or the death that is hell forever. Instead, we'll receive that gift of eternal life, or life forever in Heaven."

Reuben took a deep breath, and continued, "So, first we know we're sinners. Second, we know that the penalty or punishment for that sin is death, the final and complete separation from God. Third, we understand that Jesus paid the penalty for us and paid for the gift of eternal life, and last, we understand that if we pray, believin' with our whole heart that Jesus did that for us, we shall be saved from that punishment and receive that gift of eternal life." He looked at Estrella, saw her expression of wonder and interest, and watched as she looked from Elly to him and back to Elly.

She asked Elly, "Would you help me pray and ask for forgiveness and to receive that gift?"

Elly smiled, "I would be happy to!" She reached out for Estrella's hand, bowed her head, and led her in a simple prayer. When Estrella had asked for that forgiveness and to receive the gift of eternal life, they said Amen and wiped away some tears as they hugged one another. Reuben joined in the group hug, and they laughed together as they rose and went inside to turn in for the night.

26 / STAYOVER

Estrella was humming a tune as she came from the back room of the officer's quarters, smiling and happy as she looked at Reuben and Elly who sat at the table, steaming cups of coffee before them. Reuben rose, coffee in hand, and went to the door, stepping outside for the fresh morning air and to check on Bear who was basking in the sun. The horses had been put away in the stables and he would check on them later. He lifted his face to the rising sun, smiling and enjoying the warmth on his face. He had already spent his time with the Lord and had given considerable thought to the threatening situation with the Comanche which prompted him to plan a ride up the pass to see if the trade fair with the Comanche was as the colonel suggested. Hopefully, they would take several days which would give the Apache time to mount a defense and perhaps give the Comanche time to reconsider. But he was not very confident that would happen.

"My, you look mighty happy this morning!" declared Elly, smiling at her young friend.

"Oh, si' senora. *Estoy muy feliz*, I am very happy! Now

I know I will go to Heaven, is that not a good reason for being happy?" answered Estrella.

"Oh yes, it is, one of my favorite verses is in II Corinthians 5:17 *Therefore if any man* or woman, *be in Christ, he is a new creature; old things are passed away; behold all things are become new.* I remember when I accepted Jesus as my savior, it made so much difference in my life, and I was *a new creature.* The things I liked before, well, it was different. Now, I am happy like never before. But there will still be times when we fail Him, do wrong things, but just remember, if we go to Him and ask forgiveness, he will gladly give it to us, and take from us the burden of that sin."

Reuben stepped into the quarters just as Elly finished and the two women looked at him as he said, "The colonel has asked us to join him at the mess hall for some breakfast. Interested?"

"Yes," declared Elly, looking from Reuben to Estrella who nodded, smiling.

"Then, let's go," he said as he set his coffee cup on the table and motioned to the door.

It was a short walk across the parade ground to get to the mess hall. Several soldiers were leaving the hall and a few late arrivals were entering, all of whom noticed the women and either nodded or spoke to them. Reuben stepped aside to let the ladies enter before him. In the near corner of the hall, a rectangular table was reserved for officers and guests and the colonel stood, motioning to Elly to join him. She turned, nodded toward the colonel as she spoke to Reuben, "You sit next to him, Estrella and I will have our backs to the men, so she won't be so embarrassed."

Reuben nodded and led the way to the officer's table, extending his hand to shake the colonel's offered hand.

Reuben seated the ladies then took his seat to the right of the colonel who sat at the head of the table, which put Elly on the colonel's left directly opposite Reuben, and Estrella to her left.

"Good morning ladies!" greeted the colonel. "Thank you for gracing our table. It is not often we have so lovely a pair of ladies to join us."

"Thank you so much, Colonel. We appreciate the opportunity to enjoy a meal indoors," replied Elly, glancing around the interior of the large and simple room. With no decorations, curtains, or other embellishments, the long tables with attached benches served the utilitarian purpose. She was thankful for the individual chairs at the officers' table. They were no sooner seated than two uniformed, but aproned, men came from the serving line, one with a coffee pot and cups, the other with an armload of trays already filled with the morning's fare. The men quickly placed the trays, served the coffee, and disappeared into the kitchen area.

The trays held sausage, biscuits, gravy and at the other end, flapjacks, and syrup. Elly looked at the food, wide-eyed, "Oh my! I could never eat all this! But it looks scrumptious!"

"Well, we do have a rarity here. We have two cooks who enjoy their work, and both are quite good at it. Many men have said they never had it so good!" replied the colonel as he looked to Reuben, "Would you mind if we asked the Lord's blessing on our meal?"

"Of course not, we would be pleased if you would," answered Reuben, reaching across the table to take Estrella's hand who had already clasped Elly's. The colonel took Elly's hand, and Reuben's and began to pray a short prayer of thanks to the Lord and for blessing and protection on his guests. As he said "Amen" everyone dropped hands and reached for the utensils to enjoy the morning's fare.

As they dined, the colonel turned to Reuben, "I have stationed two men outside the post near the roadway to watch for the Comancheros, just on the off chance I could be wrong as to the time the trade fair will last, and they return sooner. I don't expect them until the end of the week, but I wanted to be certain they did not pass without stopping."

"Thank you, Colonel. I am glad to hear that. I had thought about takin' a ride up the pass and have a look myself, but perhaps that won't be necessary," replied Reuben.

Elly frowned and asked, "Comancheros?"

Reuben grinned a little, glanced to the colonel and back at Elly. "Yes, it seems there was a group of traders, Comancheros, that trade with the Comanche and other plains Indians, that passed through here the day before we arrived. It was their tracks we saw in the roadway. It seems they were on the way to have a trade fair with the Comanches. Even now, they're busy tradin' with the same bunch that hit the villages and took you two captive."

The anger flared in Elly's eyes as she looked from Reuben to the colonel and back to Reuben and asked, "Why would we wait to see the Comancheros?"

"Because one of them is Estrella's father," answered Reuben, glancing to Estrella. The girl almost spat out the food she was eating and looked wide-eyed at Reuben. She struggled to swallow and asked, "Mi Padre? But he is not a Comanchero!"

"Yes. If your father is Santiago Esquibel." He turned to the colonel and asked, "Wasn't that the man's name?"

The colonel looked from Reuben to Estrella and

nodded. "Yes. He is your father. He became a trader so he could go to the different tribes and look for you. After the raid on your home and the other homes around there, several were killed and others were taken, but you were all the family he had left, your father was determined to do all he could to get you back."

Estrella frowned. "But, what about mi Madre?"

"You didn't know? I'm sorry, but your mother was killed in the raid," answered the colonel, glancing from Reuben to Elly as if asking for help.

Elly reached her arm around Estrella's shoulder and drew her close as the girl began sobbing. Elly held her tight, whispering condolences to her as they pushed away from the table. Elly looked to Reuben, mouthed the words, "I'll take her to the quarters," and stood, to help Estrella to her feet.

As they stood, a soldier came into the hall, looked to the table for the colonel and stepped quickly to his side, saluted, and reported, "The Comancheros are coming down the road, sir. They're just coming into the open."

"Then go to them, ask Santiago Esquibel to come here, it's very important and he must come. Understood?"

"Yessir!" answered the soldier, saluting. When the colonel returned the salute, the soldier spun on his heels and quickly exited the building. The colonel looked to Elly. "If you would like, you can wait for him here, but if you prefer, I will bring the girl's father to your quarters."

Elly looked at Estrella, whose head rested on her shoulder and back to the colonel. "The quarters would be better, if you will, please."

The colonel nodded and stood, motioning to Reuben to step closer and spoke softly as the women left the building, "You might need to caution the girl. Santiago has a new wife, a part Comanche woman who was the child of a Comanche and a captured Mexican woman. I think her name is Mayte, but she will be with him."

"I understand sir. I will talk to her."

"And one other thing, did I hear you correctly that your wife and the girl were taken captive by the Comanche?" asked the colonel, frowning.

"That's right. There were several that were taken, but all were recovered."

"You got them all back?"

"That's correct. It took a little doin', but as you can see, they are safe and sound."

"And how much of the fight did you do?" asked the colonel, his head cocked to the side a mite.

"Only what was necessary. One of them, a warrior named Tosahwi took my wife and I had to convince him she was mine."

"And I'm assuming he was no longer able to argue the point?"

Reuben grinned, "That's about it."

"Good. Well, you take good care of those ladies," nodding in the direction of the retreating women.

Reuben nodded and left the mess hall, quickly joining the women as they made their way to the officers' quarters. As they walked, Reuben said, "Uh, Estrella. I know it's tough gettin' the news about your mother, but there's somethin' else you need to know. After your mother was killed, your father took another woman as his wife. I think it was because he needed her help to find you because she was the child of a Mexican woman who was taken captive and the Comanche man who kept her, and she could speak the language of the Comanche and others. Her name is Mayte."

The women had stopped walking when Reuben gave

the news, both looking at him and when he finished, Estrella frowned, shook her head, and looked at Elly. "What should I do?"

Elly smiled, hugged the girl close, and spoke softly, "It won't be easy, but she is your father's wife, and he probably loves her, which means you should learn to love her also. But don't worry about that right now, let's just get you ready to see your father again. That's the best part, isn't it?"

"Yes, there was a time I thought I would never see him again. I am very thankful for this day," answered Estrella, looking from Elly to Reuben. "And I am thankful for you two!"

27 / REUNION

"The colonel wants to see you," stated the soldier, leaning back in his saddle and pushing his cap back on his head. He glanced from the Comancheros to the other soldiers that sat with rifles across their pommels and sober faced. He saw the Comancheros, five men and one woman, look at each of the soldiers and back to the one who was speaking.

"What does he want?" asked Mateo Cardenas, the organizer and leader of the group.

The soldier, Private McIlhaney, chuckled and shook his head. He slapped his arm and asked, "Do you see any stripes here?" And moving his hand to his shoulder, "Or any bars here? No, you don't! And what that means is they don't tell me nuthin'! I just do what I'm told, and what I was told was to bring you to the colonel! So..." and gave a sweeping motion with his hand, directing them to the fort and nodded with raised eyebrows.

Mateo turned to his men, motioned to the fort, and led the entourage of six people, six horses, a dozen Indian ponies that were from the trades, and a dozen heavily laden pack mules to the adobe structures,

178

following the private and his three fellow soldiers. Private McIlhaney led them to the barn and stables to corral the animals and led the men and woman to the commandant's office. The colonel stood in the doorway watching them approach and looked at the private, "You're dismissed, Private, but first, take these others," motioning to the three men that stood to the right of Mateo, "to the mess hall and get them some coffee or whatever else they want." As the private saluted, the colonel returned the salute and turned to the Comancheros.

"So, how did your trade fair go?" he asked, directing his attention to Mateo.

The leader, glancing from the colonel to his remaining companions answered, "We had a good trade."

"Good, good. We'll talk about that, but first," he turned to Santiago Esquibel who stood frowning beside his woman, Mayte, "You, Santiago, and your woman, go to that building there," turning and directing him to the last building in the line that was clearly marked as the Officer's Quarters, "and talk to the man there, name of Reuben Grundy. He has something for you."

Santiago frowned, looked from the colonel to Mateo who nodded, and touched his hand to the elbow of his woman and they walked together toward the quarters. With a glance over his shoulder, he shook his head and mumbled something to his woman but kept walking to the building. As he approached, a man stepped into the doorway, but he was not familiar and Santiago asked, "Are you Reuben Grundy?"

"Yes, I am. You must be Santiago Esquibel, and this is your wife, Mayte?"

"Si, si, señor, but what do you want with me?"

"There's someone here you need to see," stated

Reuben as he turned to allow Santiago to see into the room. Estrella stood, hands clasped before her, head down as she peeked up to see her father.

Santiago sucked in a breath, choked on his words, as he stepped into the doorway, arms outstretched, "Mi bebé, mi pequeña niña!" and wrapped Estrella in his arms, tears streaming unbidden down his dusty cheeks. He lifted her off the ground and sat her down, leaned back to look at her and hugged her again, repeating his words again and again.

"I never thought I would find you! Where were you?" he asked as they stepped back at arm's length, looking at one another through teary eyes.

"I was taken by the Apache, until Reuben and Elly traded for me," she motioned to the two who stood near the door, Mayte beside them, "but the Comanche took all of us, including Elly there, until Reuben rescued us!"

Santiago turned to look at the man who had freed his daughter. "Oh, señor, I am so grateful, muchas gracias! I can never repay you!"

"You don't have to repay me. Estrella is our friend, and we would do anythin' for her!" answered Reuben.

Santiago's eyes fell on Mayte, and he looked back to Estrella. "This," motioning to Mayte, "is my wife, Mayte. She has helped me in the trades as I tried to find you."

"Gracias, Mayte," answered Estrella. She looked back to her father, "I did not know about mi Madre until the colonel told us." Tears came again and she dropped her forehead to her father's chest, her arms reaching around him to hold him tight.

"Would you like some coffee?" offered Elly, going to the fireplace with the coffee pot hanging near the flames. Reuben motioned everyone to the table, and grabbed the cups, setting them before each chair and sat down just as

Elly poured his cup full of the fresh coffee. She scooted a stool up to the table beside her husband and lifted her cup to her lips as she whispered to Reuben, "What about the Comanche?"

Reuben looked at Santiago who could not take his eyes from his daughter and asked, "Did you have a good trade with the Comanche?"

Santiago turned, frowned, and answered slowly, "Si, we had a good trade, why do you ask?"

"Those are the Comanche that attacked the Apache and Ute and our home. They took Estrella and my wife from our home and now they're plannin' an attack on the Apache."

"I heard talk of some planning to go after the Apache. They were glad to get the guns we had so they could make their attack."

"You traded rifles to the Comanche?" asked an incredulous Reuben, leaning forward, elbows on the table and cradling his coffee cup in his hands.

"Si, si. Why not? If they attack the Apache, what is that to me? It was the Apache that killed my wife and took my daughter! Why should you, a gringo, care what the tribes do to one another?"

Reuben gritted his teeth, his jaw muscles flexing as he glanced from Elly to Santiago. "It was also the Comanche that took your daughter from us! But if they attack the Apache, now with new rifles, there would be a slaughter of women and children as well!" He shook his head, trying to control his anger, then glared at Santiago. "What kind of rifles?"

Santiago grinned, "Mateo traded for some Confederate rifles from some deserters. They are the Springfield with paper cartridges."

"New Springfields?" asked Reuben, outraged. "Isn't there a law against sellin' rifles to the Indians?"

Santiago shrugged, glancing from his woman to Estrella and back to Reuben. "Perhaps it would be good for them to kill each other off, would it not?"

Reuben shook his head as he angrily stood and stomped from the quarters, removing himself from the presence of the man before he did something he would regret. He took long strides to the commandant's office and pushed in to find the other Comanchero, Mateo, talking with the colonel. Reuben glanced from one to the other and blurted, "Colonel, these men traded new Springfield rifles and ammunition to the Comanche! Isn't that illegal?"

"You tell me, you're the marshal?" responded the colonel.

Reuben frowned, looking from the commandant to the Comanchero and shook his head. He stuttered, "I...uh...I think so, but I don't know for sure. But it oughta be!"

"Well, until you know, there's nothing I can do. These men have a valid license to trade with the Comanche and other plains tribes. There's nothing in the licensing that prevents them trading anything." He paused, looked from Reuben to Mateo and added, "I know there have been some laws back east that forbid the natives from getting firearms, but this area is still a territory and as such, there are not yet any laws to that effect." He shrugged as he stood, turning to look out his window as was his habit whenever he was at a loss as to what to say to whoever was visiting. He turned back to the men, "Now, although I don't like the idea of arming the Comanche because I know they might choose to use those guns on us, but there's nothing I can do about it.

And you, even though you are a deputy marshal, if there's no law against it, neither can you."

Reuben shook his head, exasperated, then looked at Mateo. "Did you hear any of the Comanche talk about goin' against the Apache?"

"Yes, when I was making a trade with the war leader, Little Owl, he talked about how he could use the rifle against the Apache."

"When are they goin' to make their attack?"

"Well, I'm sure they'll spend some time getting familiar with the rifles and the ammo, but I don't think that'll take too long," replied Mateo, a slow grin splitting his face as he looked from Reuben to the colonel. He stood, reached out to shake the colonel's hand, "If there's nothing else, Colonel, we have a long way to go."

"Certainly," answered the colonel, shaking his hand and watching the man leave.

Reuben watched the Comanchero exit the office then turned to the colonel, "That's the attack I warned you about, and for the Comanche to get to the Apache, they'll come right past here."

"And if they are peaceful with us, we are bound to be peaceful with them," declared the colonel.

Reuben frowned, "So, you're of the same mind as Santiago, let the Indians kill each other and we'll be the better for it?"

The colonel took a deep breath, squinted a little showing a disapproving expression and answered, "Perhaps."

Reuben nodded, forced himself to not reply and left the colonel's office.

L ittle Owl had gathered with his recruits for the war party against the Apache. They sat on the hillside above the clearing and watched the Comancheros finish the packing of their mules, readying to leave the trade fair. Little Owl looked at his men, "The traders have many rifles, only one hand and one of our warriors gained a rifle in the trade. We need more."

"But what are we to do? The elders have said it is best to keep the traders alive, or we would have no one to trade with to get the goods we want," declared Bear Claw, a young but proven warrior that had gained many honors in the recent battles. He had quickly become a respected voice of the warriors, but he was young and by the standards of his people, inexperienced.

"There are many other traders, and they are not like these, who cheat us and demand more for their goods than they are worth! This rifle cost me all I had, and still I got very little to shoot with it!" He paused, fuming, looked around at the other warriors, "I say we take the rifles and powder from these men. They are few and will not expect us to follow them, but we must have more rifles if we are to go against the Apache!" he spat the words, contempt showing on his face as he lifted his rifle overhead and shouted his war cry. Others took up the cry as he told them to prepare to leave. They would tell the others they go against the Apache but would also take the rifles from the traders.

Of the more than twenty warriors that had agreed to go, almost half were young, most inexperienced, but all were eager for the battle and the honors to be gained. Most were as excited about the possibility of getting rifles from the traders as they were about the attack on the Apache's winter camp. As the word spread throughout the camp, the warriors gathered at the lower end of the big meadow where Little Owl waited but among those that came, was the chief, *Piarʉ Ekarʉhkapʉ*, and the Medicine Man, Isatai.

The chief scowled at Little Owl but nodded to Isatai. It was the custom of the people for the Medicine Man to pray for the warriors before they left the village that they might have a victorious battle and that all would return with great bounty. Isatai stood before the men with uplifted hands and lifted his face to the sky as he began to chant and pray, scattering pollen into the air to appease the gods. When he finished, the entire raiding party shouted their war cries and mounted their ponies, anxious for the coming fight. The chief and Medicine Man stepped aside as Little Owl led the band that now numbered close to thirty warriors, from the site of the trade fair.

Beside Little Owl rode his chosen second in command, Shave Head, a proven and respected warrior of many battles. Behind them rode Bear Claw, Buffalo Horn, and Big Mouth. Bear Claw and Big Mouth were also proven warriors, while Buffalo Horn was the lone survivor of the scouts that followed the Apache and later attacked Reuben and the women. Although Buffalo Horn had insisted it was a band of Apache, all armed with rifles, that killed his companions and left him wounded.

Shave Head asked, "Do we go past the fort?"

"No, the traders are from San Luis, and they will go south from the fort. We will go south, behind the string of mesas, scout where they are and go through the cut, or south of the mesas into the flats," answered Little Owl, picturing the area that was very familiar and had been the site of several of their buffalo hunts.

"It will be dark when we get there," observed Shave Head, looking at the sun dropping toward the mountains in the west.

"Yes, the better for our attack. They will not expect us to follow or to attack, but they have cheated our people and we will take what is ours," explained Little Owl. "They have more rifles, and only one hand of our warriors have rifles. This will make our attack on the Apache victorious." But Shave Head knew it was more than the weapons that made a raiding party return with a victory, it was the bravery and determination of their warriors and there were several with them that had yet to be proven in battle.

———————

As Reuben stomped back to the quarters, Elly saw his expression and walked out to intercept him before he lost his temper and caused some kind of ruckus. She stepped beside him, took his hand in hers and smiled up at him and said, "Take me for a walk, please." He stopped, looked down at his little woman and let a slow smile paint his face as he exhaled slowly, let his shoulders droop, and answered, "Be happy to!" and led the way as they took to a walkway that encircled the fort. The sun was high and midday had passed, but the activity of the morning had kept them from tending to the fixing of any meal, and the uncertainty of their plans added purpose to their walk.

"As Estrella and her father talked, it was good to see them together again. Between the tears and the laughter, they certainly enjoyed their reunion," said Elly, simply making conversation as they walked. She paused, looked at her man and added, "But I get the impression Estrella is uncomfortable around Mayte, and might not want to go home with them."

Reuben frowned as he looked to Elly, "But if she doesn't go home with her father, what will she do?" but he already had an idea what his wife was thinking. And that thought was made clear as she smiled up at him and suggested, "Well, she could come home with us."

"You haven't said that to her, have you? Because I wouldn't want to interfere with their family."

"Her family is not what it was, now that her mother's gone and Mayte, well, I dunno, she just doesn't seem to be too friendly or accepting of Estrella."

They began walking again, each harboring their own thoughts until Reuben asked, "Have they said anythin' about leavin', because the rest of the Comancheros won't be stayin' the night. I'm sure they'll be pullin' out anytime soon."

"They haven't said, but I guess they're waiting for word from the other traders."

"Then let's get back to the quarters and try to make sense of all this speculation," suggested Reuben, grinning at his hopeful wife.

They walked hand in hand as Elly moved closer to

her man, wrapping his arm in hers as she lifted her eyes to the sky. She shivered in the quickly cooling air and said, "I think a storm might be coming; it's getting cold!"

Reuben lifted his eyes to the sky to see big, towering clouds that seemed to be stacking themselves atop one another, the undersides showing a darkening grey, and answered, "You might be right, that could bring us some winter weather that is a little overdue. I was hopin' we'd be back home sittin by our own fireplace before that happened, but..." shrugging and reaching his arm around Elly to give her a little added warmth. They soon returned to the quarters to find Santiago talking with the leader of the Comancheros as they leaned on the hitchrail before the steps. Both men nodded to Reuben as Santiago introduced the leader, "Reuben and Elly, this is Mateo Cardenas. He organized this trade with the Comanche."

Reuben extended his hand, shook with Mateo, as he said, "Good to meet you, Mateo. You fellas gettin' ready to pull out?" he asked.

"Si, si. We will be leaving shortly. The colonel offered for us to take a meal with the soldados before we leave, and the others were happy to do so. We will take the meal and leave right after. It is too far to make it to San Luis before nightfall, so we will camp along the way." He shrugged and added, "It is the life of the trader." He looked to Santiago, "You know the cut between the mesas where the Trinchera creek flows? That is where we will camp tonight. It is not too far but will get us closer to San Luis and tomorrow will be easy traveling. You will be home before dark tomorrow."

Estrella had come to the door when she heard Reuben's voice and as Mateo explained their plans, she asked her father, "Could we stay here tonight? We can make San Luis in one day, can we not?"

Santiago had also noticed the clouds and the chill in the air, looked from Estrella to Mateo. "We *will* stay here tonight and leave early in the morning. We will probably catch up to you before you get to San Luis, but if not, you can leave my share of the trade goods at my place."

"We can do that, but the horses, do you want to keep one for your daughter?" asked Mateo.

"Yes, any one will do, they are all good animals. The others you can leave in my corral."

Mateo nodded, turned away and without a word, moved past Reuben and Elly to return to his men. Elly motioned to Estrella and the women went into the quarters while Reuben and Santiago sat on the bench outside. Santiago had been fussing with a pipe, stuffing the bowl with tobacco, and readying it to be lit. He lifted it to his mouth, struck a lucifer on the wall and puffed deep to light the tobacco. Exhaling a big cloud, he looked over to Reuben and asked, "Do you have any children?"

"No, we don't. We've only been married a short while and haven't really settled down long enough to consider makin' a family."

"My daughter said you have a cabin in the valley beyond the mountains. Have you been there long?"

"No, it's new. This will be our first winter there."

They sat quiet for a while until Santiago said, "I think my daughter does not want to come home. And, my woman, she's, well, she's not sure about having another woman in the house."

Reuben turned to look at the man, "But, she's your daughter. Don't you want her home?"

"Si, si. But the little girl I searched for, she is gone, and in her place is this young woman. Her mother is also gone, and I do not know what to do with a young woman!" declared Santiago, shaking his head. "I am happy she is safe because my heart has been so empty and I have been so angry and afraid, but now..." he shrugged, unable to explain further. "Where we live, there are only old men, farmers, and such, that have lost their women and would take another. But there are no young men that would be suitable for her."

"Well, I think my wife would like to have her come home with us. She was gettin' used to havin' her as part of our family and, well, it was good for my wife to have the company."

"Are there any men that would be a suitable husband for her?" asked Santiago, hopeful.

Reuben grinned, "Not a one. But she's still young and there's no tellin' what the next few years might show. We're not too far from the new settlement they're callin' Cañon City, and there's always the prospect of new settlers comin' into the valley, makin' ranches and such."

"And we could come visit?" asked Santiago.

"Certainly, anytime," answered Reuben. "But for right now, how 'bout we go get us some dinner?"

The women stepped through the door just as the men rose and Reuben said, "Well, just in time. Let's go get us some dinner and maybe talk about things, alright?" as he winked at Elly.

Elly smiled and slipped her hand through Reuben's crooked arm as they led the way to the Mess Hall for the meal together.

Dusk was shaking out her skirts of light, leaving the world in a pale shadow as the Comancheros made camp beside the Trinchera creek. The willows were thick beside the water while a smattering of gnarled cottonwood stretched their bony silhouettes into the fading light as if trying to snatch light from the darkness. The four men had managed to fashion a rope corral to keep the horses and mules from wandering. It had been quite a task for the men to handle the many horses traded from the Comanche and their own animals, including the pack mules. Mateo stood beside the rope looking at the animals and frowned, "That palomino was not a part of our herd, where'd she come from?"

"There were two of them at the stables, this one kept coming around the bunch we traded from the Comanche. I think she might have been with them before, so..." shrugged Sebastian Ochoa.

Mateo scowled at the man, "If the soldados discover she is gone before we are well away, they will come after us!"

"I don' think she was one of the soldados, mebbe one

of those that had Santiago's daughter, but not the soldados," suggested Sebastian. Their talk had brought the
other two men, Alejandro and Candelario, beside them.
Sebastian looked to them, eyes pleading for their
support.

"I think he is right, Mateo. The hombre with Santiago's daughter had other horses there, and the other
palomino was his, so..." suggested Alejandro.

"Are we going to leave the horses and other goods at
Santiago's home, or keep them?" asked Sebastian,
changing the thoughts and grinning with lust.

"Hah! We only needed him for his license, and he got
what he wanted, his daughter. We will keep the rest
ourselves," muttered Mateo, kicking at a stick at his feet.

Mateo scowled at them all, shaking his head, and
started back to the fire ring. This site had been used
before by other travelers, Indian and traders alike, and
the fire ring had blackened and partially burned wood,
but little enough for a fire. Mateo hollered to the others,
"Alejandro, fetch some firewood! Sebastian, secure the
packs and bring a coffee pot! Candelario, get the bedrolls
and lay them out!" He continued to mumble to himself,
but knew his companions were the only ones that dared
travel with him into the camps of the different Indian
tribes, each time putting their lives in danger, although
the trades had been profitable. This last trip was not as
good as he hoped, but it was good to go into the winter
with an ample stock of trade goods and many horses and
other plunder to pass on to the merchants in Santa Fe.

With the late meal at the fort, the men only wanted
some coffee to warm them before turning in for the
night. The air had turned cool and was whispering
through the cut between the timbered mesas that sided
the little stream. But there was better shelter here with

the trees and the buttes and mesas, compared to trying to find shelter among the sage and greasewood in the flats. Tomorrow they would make San Luis, perhaps further, and there were many farms that would offer their barns for shelter. It would be another week before reaching Santa Fe, but the appeal of the town and warm beds would be ample reward for their labors.

Their bedrolls were in the open, arrayed around the fire ring, the nearby cottonwoods offering a wind break, and the men snuggled down beneath the blankets. Mateo looked at the stars, but the southern sky was dark with heavy clouds and few stars shone through the thick cover. He rolled to his side, pulling the blankets over his shoulder, and trying to get comfortable as they lay on the low cropped grasses.

———

THE SNOW BEGAN SHORTLY AFTER DEEP DARKNESS enveloped the camp. Light fluffy flakes drifted to the ground silently laying its downy blanket of white on the Creator's handiwork. The big flakes sparkled in the light of the silvery moon as it peeked from the heavy clouds. The sleeping forms became mounds of white that differed little from the surroundings.

The Comanche scouts had told Little Owl of the location of the camp of the traders, and the warriors rode with blankets around their shoulders as they moved behind the big buttes, going to the trail beside Trinchera Creek. Little Owl gathered his leaders around him, giving them the orders for their attack on the camp. "No rifles! This will be done silently!" he demanded as he looked from Shave Head to Bear Claw. The men nodded, turned away to take their chosen warriors to encircle the camp and take their vengeance.

The first arrow came from Bear Claw's bow, whispering through the falling snow to bury itself in the back of Alejandro Fuentes. The man arched his back from the impact, throwing off the blankets as he struggled and moaned, trying to warn the others, but his efforts were in vain. Two other arrows came from Shave Head's warriors, finding their target in the chest of Candelario and Mateo Cardenas. But Mateo sat up, the arrow buried deep in his shoulder and shouted, "Indians!" But his cry fell on deaf ears as Buffalo Horn had buried his tomahawk in the head of Alejandro, splitting his scalp and spraying blood across the new fallen snow. Another arrow whispered through the air, plunging deep into the throat of Mateo, driving him to his back, painting the snow with blood that pumped from his throat as Mateo choked to death.

Silence lingered over the camp, all the traders were dead, and the Comanche walked into the clearing. Little Owl shouted orders to the warriors, "Shave Head, Bear Claw, find the rifles and bullets! Big Mouth, Buffalo Horn, move the horses onto the trail. Lone Walker, you and one man, take the horses back to our village!"

Lone Walker looked at his war leader, shaking his head as he pleaded, "Send another, I must have vengeance on the Apache! I had a woman, but they took her back!"

Little Owl looked at the man, knowing a warrior seeking vengeance would be a better fighter than a young untested man. He nodded to Lone Walker, turned to the others, and said, "Black Horse, you and one other, take the horses back to the village."

Black Horse nodded, pointed his lance at one of the

untested young men that he knew was good with horses, and said, "You, Broken Shield, we will take the horses!" The young man's shoulders drooped, but he looked at Black Horse and nodded, turning his mount toward the rope corral and the gathered horses and mules. The Comanche had little use for the mules, but perhaps they could be used for trade, and the two men pushed the small herd of more than a dozen horses and about the same number of mules, to the narrow trail that would take them back over the same trail they followed to the traders' camp.

In the dim light and snow, the narrow trail through the cut was difficult for the two men to move well over twenty animals. They were huddled under blankets, disappointment at missing out on the impending attack on the Apache hindering their attention to the herd and neither man saw the palomino cut back into a cluster of juniper. When three stubborn mules ducked into the willows, the two men showed little concern and no desire to chase after the recalcitrant beasts. They pushed the herd through the cut and out of the timber as the trail broke into the open in the wide park that lay behind the timbered mesas. The wind had picked up and the blowing snow drove the herd into the trees at the base of the buttes. When the two men looked at one another, a simple nod said they would take shelter, build a fire, and wait out the storm. The horses were of less concern than their own survival.

———

ESTRELLA AND HER FATHER WALKED IN SILENCE, ARM IN arm, huddled in their heavy coats against the cold and snow. The night's storm had dropped no more than five or six inches of snow, but the constant wind had drifted the white fluff into the corners and against the walls of the fort, around the trees and bushes, but leaving the walkway clear. A quick glance to the sky told Santiago there would be more snow and the storm was just gathering its strength for a much bigger drop. They crossed the roadway to get to the barn and corrals, but Santiago frowned and looked at the pole fence where a wet palomino stood, looking at the horses huddled against the barn wall. He glanced from the horse to his daughter as she walked toward the yellow horse, hand outstretched and talking softly to the animal.

"Is that your horse?" asked Santiago, frowning.

"Si, si. This is the one Reuben traded for from the Apache. I rode her and liked her," she said as she began stroking the animal's face. It was evident the two had a connection as the horse pushed against her hand. "But why is she out here?"

"Maybe I can answer that," came a voice from the open barn door. "I was just comin' to get her and let her in with the others. She was taken by them traders. They gathered her up with their horses they got from the Comanch. But looks like she cut loose from 'em and came back. I reckon she's been runnin' through the snow to get back to you, missy." The soldier moved closer with a halter and started putting it on the palomino. He handed Estrella the lead line, "You can lead her into one of the stalls there next to them other horses of that fella that you came in with. Be sure to rub her down good, get that wet off her coat and let her dry out a mite. She's a good horse."

"Were you on guard when the traders left?" asked Santiago.

"Yeah, I purty much stay here in the barn. I'm the

smithy for the horses an' such," answered the uniformed man.

"Then why did they take this horse?" asked Santiago.

"Well, that one fella said he traded for it. I reckon he fancied it and wanted it for his own self. There was nobody here to argue 'bout it so I reckoned he was bein' truthful. Didn't 'spect nobody to try to steal a horse right in front o' me," declared the smithy, shaking his head and jamming his hands in his pockets. He lifted his eyes to the sky, "I'm thinkin' we're in for a big 'un!"

He looked at Santiago, "Say, weren't you one o' them?"

"Si, si. But I stayed here after I found my daughter. She had been taken by the Apache and I had looked for her many times, but the gringo brought her to me," answered Santiago.

"Then maybe you'd be interested to know, three o' them pack mules followed this palomino back here. I got 'em in the back corral yonder," shared the smithy, motioning to the corrals behind the barn. "Can't figger that 'un. I reckon somethin' bad had to happen for them mules to be wanderin' loose."

Santiago frowned, looking at the smithy and watching Estrella take the palomino into the barn. "I am taking my horses and the one pack mule and going home to San Luis today. I can take those mules with me and return them to the others."

"Suits me, but this shore don't seem to be travelin' weather," stated the smithy, going back into the barn to get out of the wind.

Santiago led his mount and the string of runaway mules while Estrella led Mayte's horse and the one pack mule of her father's. As they wrapped leads around the hitch rail in front of the quarters, Reuben stood in the doorway and asked, "I thought you said you had one pack mule, did you buy some more?"

"No. These were the mules of Mateo and the others. They will need them to pack the trade goods, but they ran away, followed her," nodding to Estrella, "palomino back to the barn."

Reuben frowned, "What was the palomino doin' loose?"

"I think Alejandro wanted her and took her. He told the smithy he traded for her and took her with their other horses."

Reuben shook his head, looking from Santiago to the mules, "You think somethin' happened?"

Santiago nodded his head, "Si, but I do not know what."

"Did they trade all the rifles they had to the Comanche?"

"No, they had many more, but the Comanche had little to trade with and Mateo kept the rifles for another time."

"I'm thinkin' the Comanche didn't want to wait for another time. I'd be willin' to bet they took those rifles," declared Reuben.

antiago and Reuben rode side by side, faces into the light snow. Reuben had volunteered to join Santiago, leaving the women at the fort, until they could discover what happened to the traders. The rising sun off their left shoulder cast a rosy glow on the white blanket that lay quietly on the flats. Wind drove the flakes from the southeast, whistling and howling as it fell from the heights of the buttes and mesas, stacking in drifts upon the sage and greasewood. Clumps of buffalo grass and cacti caught the drifting white, stacking it around their roots as if blanketing their bases with winter's supply of moisture, to hoard it until needed at a later time. The horses tucked their muzzles against their chest, laying their ears back against their necks and manes to protect against the blistering cold.

The campsite of the Comancheros was about four miles south of the fort, marked by the cut that showed as the long shadows of the mesas split to reveal the morning light that stabbed through the break. A brief pause in the wind allowed Reuben and Santiago to turn into the campsite, known and used by Santiago on previous trade ventures.

The Comanche had focused their efforts on the packs and trade goods, scattering the unnecessary gear and goods aside like useless litter. The bodies of the traders, frozen in place, drifting snow giving the appearance of graceful sculptures. Reuben walked among the dead, looked at the stoic face of Santiago, "We won't be able to bury them. The ground is frozen and so are the bodies," declared Reuben.

"It is of no matter. They were thieves and would have stolen all I had, but I did not care for I found Estrella. They had stolen her horse and would have stolen what should have been my share, but it did not matter. But I would not wish this upon anyone," muttered Santiago as he rummaged through the remaining trade goods.

Reuben had spotted the broken arrows that still protruded from two of the bodies and they knew it was the Comanche that had killed the traders. He walked around the camp, saw the remains of the rope corral, the sign of the horses taking the trail back to the village, but also the sign of the warriors headed directly west. They had apparently stayed in the camp with the dead bodies until the break in the storm near daybreak, then started west apparently to the Apache encampment. He looked to Santiago. "Do you know where the winter encampment of the Apache lies?"

"Si, we have been there on a trade venture, when I was searching for my daughter. But when I was there, many had left for the spring buffalo hunt and my daughter was not there, nor did anyone tell me of her."

"How long would it take the Comanche to get there, assumin' they left at daylight today?" asked Reuben.

"Two days, but leaving this morning, it would be

dark or close before they made the encampment and the second day. They would not attack with tired horses and men. They would wait until the next mañana!"

"Then I still have time!" stated Reuben. "Will you ride back to the fort and let the women know what I am doin'?"

"Si, but do you not want me to go with you?"

"I can make better time by myself, and the women would worry if they do not know what I am doing."

"Si, I comprendo. I will do as you ask. But what can you, one man, do to stop the many Comanche?"

"Whatever I can. I cannot abide a surprise attack that will kill many women and children. If this was just a battle between warriors, then I might stay out of it. But after I learned of the treatment the women would get if they were taken captive," he shook his head without further alluding to what he knew, but grabbed up the reins of Blue, and swung aboard.

"If you follow the creek," began Santiago, pointing to the meandering Trinchera Creek that had carved its way into the flats of the wide valley, "stay on the north bank. When you see several buttes to the north, go to them, stay on the north side, and go straight to the Rio Bravo del Norte, cross over. If you can see in this storm," he glanced to the sky and the storm that appeared to be increasing, "keep going due west. There will be a cut in the mountains where a stream splits the mountains. There is the encampment."

Reuben nodded, "Well, I'm thinkin' it's time for a little reparation. A little payback is just what these Comanche need to be doin'. They've stolen, killed, destroyed, and now the bill is comin' due." He reined Blue around and started what would be a cold and desperate journey, hopefully one that would save many lives.

Santiago watched as Reuben disappeared into the blowing and drifting snow, then mounted up to return to the fort. Any remains of the trade goods would not be going anywhere, and he could return with pack mules and gather up the scattered remains when the weather subsided. For now, it was important for him to tell his daughter and Elly of Reuben's determination to help the Apache.

———————

ELLY, ESTRELLA, AND MAYTE WERE WALKING ACROSS THE parade ground on their way back to the quarters, their heads ducked to shield their faces from the blowing snow, when Santiago rode into the grounds, and stepped down to tether his horse at the hitchrail. When Elly saw the man was alone, she was alarmed and hurried to his side. "Where's Reuben?" she asked, fearful of the answer.

"He is alright, but let's talk," he said, motioning to the door of the quarters. They quickly entered, stomping the snow from their feet, and stripping off their coats and scarves, stepping close to the fireplace and stretching out cold hands to absorb the warmth.

Elly looked at Santiago, "Alright, tell me!" she demanded.

Santiago began with their discovery and their assumptions based on the remaining sign at the camp. "He is bound to the Apache encampment. He believes he must help them. He spoke of what he knew about the captive women and others and was determined to not let that happen. I tried to talk him out of it, but he is *muy terco*, very stubborn!"

Elly could not help but smile at his expression, nodding her head in agreement. She dropped her eyes, turned back to face the fire and holding out her hands again and staring into the flames, she considered what she thought Reuben would expect her to do, obviously it was to stay at the fort, but with her man riding into danger, she could not just sit back and do nothing. She looked at Santiago and Estrella, "I must go to him. He needs my help. One man against so many..." she shook her head at the thought. She looked at Santiago, "The rifles that were traded to the Comanche, what kind?"

"Springfields, like the soldados use in the war."

"But they are single shot muzzle loaders, right?"

"Si, si. But they are faster than most others," offered Santiago, frowning as he looked at this woman that stood beside his daughter. The one who had committed to keep his daughter and help her as she blossomed into womanhood.

Elly looked at Estrella, "You should stay here. The colonel will make sure you are safe."

Estrella let a slow grin split her face, "If you go, I go. I can help, but I will need a rifle."

Santiago added, "And if Estrella goes, I will go also."

Mayte had been silent and frowned at Santiago. She asked, "Why do you go? These are Apache, the ones who killed your wife and took your daughter. Why would you go to help them?"

Santiago dropped his eyes, "It is because of what Reuben said, it is not who they are that matters. It is wrong for them to take the women from their families, or to kill the women and children. It is not because they are Apache or Comanche. As Reuben said, if it was just a fight between warriors, then let them fight. But it is a raid that will cause many women and children to die or be taken away from their homes and family. The families will feel as I did when my wife was killed, and my daughter taken. No one should have that."

"Then I will go too. Mi Madre suffered that with the Comanche, but she lived to give me life. She tried many times to escape and was killed by the Comanche. Even though my father was a Comanche warrior, he was not a good man. I will go with you!" she declared, setting her jaw in determination as she looked at Santiago. The man was surprised at her decision but pleased. He did not want either his woman or his daughter to be put into danger, but he was resolved to do the right thing.

"What kind of rifles do you have?" asked Elly, looking from Santiago to Mayte.

"I have the same rifles as those we traded, the Springfield," stated Santiago, proudly.

Elly frowned, "My husband taught me one thing, when we are outnumbered, we can even the odds if we have better weapons. I saw what we need at the sutler's. If you and Estrella will go to the stables and get our horses ready, I will go to the sutler's and see what I can get."

Santiago nodded, motioning for both Estrella and Mayte to come with him. Elly gathered up her coat and started to the sutler, thinking about the rifles she had seen when they first came to the fort. Perhaps she could improve the odds with the right weapons.

E lly was digging through their gear, getting out anything that would keep them warm and dry. She had a heavy capote and a union suit she would don, and as she looked through the packs, a paper fluttered to the floor. She frowned as she bent to pick it up and saw it was a telegram. Reuben had mentioned something about the telegrapher holding a telegram but she forgot all about it. She slipped it from the envelope and began to read,

> *Marshals Grundy*
> *Points south*
> *Upon receipt of this message, contact the office of Governor Evans. In urgent need of marshals in South Park and surrounding area. Confederate rebels causing trouble with the gold shipments needed by the union.*
> *John Evans*
> *Governor, Colorado Territory*

"Well, I can understand why he wasn't anxious to respond to this!" she mumbled as she jammed the missive into her pocket and continued searching for warm clothing.

As Elly exited the quarters, Santiago and the other women stood by the horses and pack mule. The mule was loaded with packs provided by Elly, and carried food, cooking gear, and extra blankets. She went to her appaloosa and strapped her bedroll on behind the cantle; she was wearing her buckskin leggings and tunic over the union suit with the red and black capote over her shoulders. She swung aboard her saddle and started to turn away, but looked at Santiago, "You know where we're going, so you better lead out!"

He nudged his bay gelding beside her and pointed to the west and south, "I think if we go to the southwest, we will cut their trail. He was bound due west, would cross the Trinchera Creek and head for the buttes, the only high ground in the valley."

"That sounds like him. But with this blowing snow, are we going to have problems?"

"No, I don't think so, señora. It is blowing and drifting, but not too much fresh snow is falling. If the wind lets up, it will be better. Reuben can follow the sign of the Comanche easy, even with the snow. They did not have a big lead on him and if he does like I think he will, he could get past them, if he wants."

"Then I think we should head for those same buttes. We might have to travel some after dark, but if it's not too cloudy, the moon is still big and we could see alright," suggested Elly. She looked down at Bear, motioned for him to stay close and watched as Santiago took the lead.

———

FOLLOWING THE TRAIL OF THE COMANCHE WAS EASY enough for Reuben, even though the snow was blowing and filling the tracks. Whenever twenty or more horses pass, they leave ample sign, not just the tracks and turned soil, but droppings and cropped grass and more. Reuben nudged Blue to a canter, wanting to gain as much ground as possible before nightfall. He guessed he was no more than two or three hours behind, believing they left their camp about the same time as he and Santiago left the fort. With the camp no more than four miles south of the fort, he guessed the Comanche to be about that same distance ahead of him.

He reached down and stroked the side of Blue's neck, "Good boy! You and your long legs should be able to catch up to those Comanche soon enough." He sat upright, pulled his collar up, his hat down, and hunched his shoulders to keep out the wind. He trusted Blue and his surefooted gait as he squinted his eyes from the cold. He was thinking about what Santiago said about a series of buttes and mesas that marked the south edge of the trail, if he made time and could swing around those buttes, he might get ahead of the Comanche and use the high ground to his advantage. Even the weather could be in his favor, but if the snow was too thick and the wind too strong, his scope on the Sharps would be useless. He shook his head at the thought and leaned into the wind.

Reuben slowed Blue, giving him a breather as they cut through some tall sage that gave a little break from the incessant wind and blowing snow. Whenever the sun pushed through the clouds, Reuben gauged the time, knowing he had been on the move for at least two hours, maybe three. He had been riding on the south side of Trinchera Creek and now saw the tracks of the Comanche angle slightly north of west and pointed to the creek. They were probably going to the water for their horses and maybe a midday break for food or to rest the horses. Reuben chose to continue west, hoping to cross the creek lower and maybe make the buttes ahead of the war party. If he did get ahead of them, he knew they would not be alarmed at a single rider, especially in the blowing snow.

After crossing the creek and pushing through the willows, he kicked Blue into a canter again, anxious to get to the buttes before the Comanche. He was asking a lot of the roan, but the horse was eager to please his rider and easily stretched out to his ground eating gait. The wind was coming off his left shoulder and was intermittent, but cold. Blue's mane waved in the wind, his tail was lifted, his ears laid back, his head stretched out as he cut through the blowing snow.

Shadows began to loom in the distance, vague humps in the terrain, everything was the same dull white, and it was hard to make out the shapes, yet Reuben had kept a close look on the trail, watching for any sign of the Comanche and he was certain he was ahead of them, but time was short.

He pulled Blue back to a walk, determined to keep the roan from breaking into a heavy sweat that would freeze and do them both in, and a cluster of tall sage showed itself, offering temporary sanctuary. He reined in his horse, slipped to the ground, and grabbed a corner of a blanket from his pack, cut it off and began rubbing Blue down. The horse leaned into his hand, enjoying, and appreciating the rub down, and Reuben basked in the closeness of the warm horse and shelter of the sage. Once finished, he started out, leading Blue behind him, and covering ground with his long strides, his chin tucked into his collars.

An occasional glance showed the buttes ahead and he stopped, looking around in all directions, searching for the war party, but the now gusting wind, still lifted the snow and tossed it about, making visibility limited. Stepping back aboard Blue, he nudged his mount forward, pointing to the slope nearest the creek, planning on encircling the buttes, keeping them between him and the Comanche until he could gain the high ground and choose his firing position.

Once on the lee side of the smaller hillock, he started around the back side, staying well out of the wind. As he circled them, he was reminded of the many anthills he used to see, pointed mounds made of tiny bits of gravel, one or two entry holes, and ants all about. These hills and buttes looked just like giant anthills, although not as perfectly formed, and the only rocks were near the crest. Mostly covered by bunch grass or buffalo grass, and rabbit brush, the mounds seemed out of place in the vast flatlands of the San Luis Valley, but they stood watch over the lowlands just the same.

The wind abated and Reuben scampered up the nearest butte, bellying down at the crest and searched for the Comanche. They were easily seen, the band of more than twenty warriors, bunched up for protection from the wind, they looked like a giant centipede crawling toward the cover of the mesas and buttes where Reuben waited. He guessed them to be no more than three or four miles out, moving at a walk and coming directly toward him.

He quickly scanned the hills around him, searching for the best promontory and chose one humpback ridge that held rocks and scrub oak on top that would provide good cover. He quickly crabbed back from the crest, took the slope in long leaping strides, and snatched up the reins of Blue, swung aboard and kicked him to quickly cross the low saddle between two buttes and go to cover behind the ridge. He loosely tied Blue in a little sandy bottomed runoff gulch that had blown clear of snow and showed a bit of grass as it lay at the base of the ridge, grabbed his Henry and Sharps, the saddle bags, and binoculars, and hotfooted it up the steep slope of the humpback ridge.

He spotted the perfect site, a wide flat limestone slab, covered with lichen and moss, sitting beside a scrub piñon and some scrub oak brush. He dropped behind it, lay out the rifles and saddle bags, then picked up the binoculars for a quick look before the wind kicked up again. He grinned as he saw a familiar face, one of the men that was at the fight with the Apache and was guarding the women but left before the others. Beside him was none other than the runaway that tried to attack him and his women as they followed the Apache. He was the one they patched up and set him free. Reuben shook his head, pulled the Sharps up close and lay out several paper cartridges. "Reparation time, boys, you need to pay back for what you done!" he whispered as he lifted the rifle to his shoulder, sighted through the scope, judged the Comanche to be about four to four hundred fifty yards away and adjusted his aim accordingly. He narrowed his sight on the leader, who rode with a blanket around his shoulders, a war shield in front, and a lance laying across the withers of his mount. Reuben lowered his aim to the edge of the war shield, knowing it would probably knock the man off his horse, maybe break an arm, but it was not a kill shot.

He eared back the hammer, placed a cap on the nipple, sighted through the scope as he eared the hammer to full cock, and lightly placed his finger on the thin forward trigger and began to squeeze. The big Sharps bucked and roared, spitting lead and smoke, but even before the bullet found its mark, Reuben dropped the lever, opening the breech to eject the remains of the paper and slid another paper cartridge up the groove and into the breech. He closed the breech by lifting the lever, cutting off the back end of the paper to expose the powder. He brought the hammer to half-cock, placed a cap on the nipple and brought the rifle back to his shoulder to sight through the scope, bringing the hammer to full cock.

As he looked at the war party, they were scattering in every direction, the leader was on the ground, but moving and shaking his head. Another warrior came close, covering his leader with his horse, and looking in the direction of the mounds. But they were too far away for their reckoning, and they searched the nearby sage, but another bull roar filled the plains, and the second warrior was spilled from his mount, the bullet cutting through his buffalo robe and crushing his ribs as it tore through his chest. The man landed in a clump of prickly pear cactus but did not move.

Reuben knew they had not yet spotted him, the pale grey smoke blending with the blowing snow and overcast plus the distance was further than they considered possible. Suddenly the entire band spread out, charging at the sage and greasewood, believing the shooter to be among the brush. They jabbed at the brush with their lances, screaming their war cries, running their mounts through the thick greasewood brush, cutting up their legs, but showing no mercy to the animals. Blood was splattered on the drifted snow, horses were rearing and pawing at the sky, trying to unseat their vicious riders, warriors were shouting and screaming, but no one found the shooter. Reuben moved to another big rock, laid out his Henry and shouldered his Sharps. He picked another target, a man near the downed leader, who stood beside him, looking about at his warriors and the pandemonium of the horses and riders. Reuben squeezed off another shot, but just as he did, one of the runaway horses jumped in front and the bullet drove through the animal's chest, causing him to stumble and fall to the side, almost burying the standing target underneath.

Two more warriors came to the side of their leader, started to pull him away from the melee and behind some sage, but Reuben dropped the hammer again and one man's head exploded, spraying blood and detritus on the nearby warrior, as he crumpled to the ground. The second warrior dropped behind the dead horse, looking about for the shooter, but saw nothing revealing. He shouted to the leader, "It is a ghost! He rides the wind and kills our warriors! We cannot see him!" Others heard what the man shouted, passed it on, and most of the others dropped to the ground, crawling behind sage and greasewood for cover.

T he wind had let up considerably, but the overcast still hindered visibility. Elly and the Esquibels had ridden hard and fast, hopeful of catching Reuben before any conflict started with the Comanche. Bear trotted beside Elly and the appaloosa, although she had named the horse, Daisy, she seldom used the term when talking to the animal, more often using the pet name 'girl'. She leaned down and stroked the appy's neck, talking to her as they rode, "Sorry to ride you so hard, girl, but we've got to get to Reuben before those Comanche. You understand, don't you, girl?" She sat upright, squinting her eyes as she searched the flats before them, seeing nothing but the clumps of sage, greasewood, and the smaller mounds of rabbit brush and buffalo grass. The snow had been blown around and heaped against anything and everything it would cling to, giving the flatlands a white freckled appearance.

The only advantage was the dampness of the dry grasses and other undergrowth that quieted the footfalls of the horses, helping the four to move silently through the countryside. The wind still whistled and moaned, pausing a few moments, then picking up again. As they traveled, a quick glance at the seldom appearing sun told Elly it was mid to late afternoon, and they had been traveling continuously. They would have to stop soon, let the horses get some water and rest, before continuing. She suddenly reined up, leaning into the wind that came from the south, glanced to Santiago, "Did you hear that?"

Before he could answer, "There! That's Reuben's big Sharps! The fight's already started!"

Santiago had come alongside Elly; they had traded off taking the lead and he had fallen back with Mayte while Estrella sided Elly. Now he put a hand behind one ear, "I heard what sounded like a gunshot!"

"That's Reuben's Sharps! It doesn't crack, it blasts with a roar! We've got to get up there!"

She started to kick her appy into action until Santiago stopped her, "No! You could run right into the Comanche, and they would kill you!" he declared. "We must be careful. Let me go first, I know the land. There is a bit of a gully that we can use, if I can find it in this snow!" he kicked his bay into a trot then a canter. The others followed close behind, Elly shaking her head, her heart ready to pound its way out of her chest. The appy stretched out her neck, matching the bay stride for stride, while Estrella and Mayte lay low on their horses' necks, the manes slapping at their faces and the wet cold making the mane feel like icicles against their skin.

The gully showed itself and Santiago led the foursome into the sandy bottomed draw. The sides were like shelves of mud and dirt that held rocks and roots within its dry soil. The storm came from the south, the gully stretched north to south, and the banks offered cover with scattered sage clinging to the edges of the washout. The banks were high enough to shield the horses, and

Santiago quickly dropped to the ground and went to the bank that faced the flats where the Comanche were gathered.

A slight rise stood between them and the war party, shielding them completely from their view. Elly looked about, saw the buttes to her right and knew Reuben was somewhere atop them; it was his way to find the high ground. As she looked, she heard the boom of his rifle and spotted the quickly dissipating smoke that disappeared into the overcast of the storm. She smiled, knowing he was safe, at least for now.

Elly looked at Santiago as he turned to face the women, "That rise is just what we need. There's plenty of sage and greasewood for cover, and we can fall back to the draw. The war party is just on the other side, and we can have a bit of advantage with that rise above them." Elly nodded, "I saw where Reuben is, atop that humpback ridge there. I'm sure he will see us, but if not, once we start shooting, he'll know it's us."

"Then let's take our positions. Once there, do not shoot until I do. Try to make your shots count and space them out, maybe move around some to make them think there are more of us." He paused, lifted the new Henry that Elly had bought, one for each of them. "With these, we can do a lot of shooting."

Estrella was close beside Elly, while Mayte was beside Santiago. He looked from one to the other, "We," motioning to Mayte, "will go to this end," pointing to the left edge of the rise, "You two, space out on that end, but stay close enough so you can protect one another." With a nod, he climbed the bank and started up the slope in a crouch, keeping as low as possible. Mayte mimicked his moves, staying within ten to fifteen feet behind him. They no sooner started running than Elly and Estrella did the same to the top of the rise, keeping a clump of sage between them and the Comanche.

They dropped to their bellies, one on either side of the sage, and Elly spoke softly, "Pick your targets and squeeze, don't jerk, the trigger. Then jack another round in and do it again."

Estrella nodded, "I have wanted to do this ever since they took us," she said, eyes squinted and a slight snarl curling her lip.

Bear had followed and now lay on his belly beside Elly, a low growl rumbling deep in his chest. The first shot of Santiago startled Elly and Estrella, but they quickly recovered, picked their targets, and cut loose.

The Comanche had taken cover behind the bigger clumps of sage, trying to shield their horses from the shooter that was somewhere to the south of them, but the rise was to their west, off their right shoulder and every warrior was exposed. The first barrage from the four shooters stunned the warriors, killing two and wounding another. The shouting and scampering would have been humorous to watch if it was not more of a death dance than a celebratory display. The second barrage was staggered, but the number of shots also surprised the Comanche. The wounded Little Owl shouted, "There are too many! Shoot them!"

Staggered shots came from the Comanche, but they were not familiar with the new rifles and had chosen not to waste any of the ammunition in practice. Now the idea of tearing open a paper cartridge was confusing to them, even those that had previously used a muzzle loading flintlock. The paper cartridges had to be torn open, which soldiers were taught to do by using their teeth, the powder put down the muzzle, the enclosed Minié ball pushed into the muzzle, and all pushed down the barrel with the ramrod. Then a cap had to be put on the nipple below the half-cocked hammer, then the hammer brought to full cock, aim and fire.

Some of the warriors struggled with the paper cartridge, others with the cap, several accidentally fired the rifle before bringing it to their shoulder, and those that succeeded with the many steps, could not hit what they were aiming at, and most often did not even come close. All the while they were struggling with their loading and more, bullets were cutting through the brush and hitting many of the warriors. Bloody bodies lay askew against the low snowdrifts, painting the drift with their blood.

Within moments, Little Owl was shouting at his warriors, "Get to your horses! We must leave here now!" Two men helped Little Owl to move through the thick brush, his horse tethered beside a large clump of sage. They hoisted him aboard and quickly ran to their own horses, but before they made it, one was dropped by a bullet from Santiago, and Elly had taken the measure of Little Owl and dropped the hammer on her Henry, sending a bullet through the neck of the war leader. Blood splattered on his horse's neck, the smell of the blood startling the horse that reared up, pawed at the clouds, and dumped the body of Little Owl into the rabbit brush, before tucking his head between his front hooves and kicking at the wind with his hind hooves. The black horse bucked and kicked, whinnying his protests, as he split the brush and disappeared into the overcast that lay low on the flats.

The few survivors fled the flats, clinging tenaciously to the manes of their horses, many were wounded and bleeding and would die before making it to the main trail. The others kept riding, their horses at a full gallop, to escape the carnage that came upon them. They would tell the tale of the ghost killer and the hundred warriors that fired on them, killing their fellow warriors, bringing shame to the great Comanche, making them flee for their lives.

The melee before them caused Elly and company to hold their fire as they watched the terrified warriors flee for their lives. When all was still before them, Santiago motioned to the rest to return to the draw. Everyone crabbed back from the crest, refusing to expose themselves to any Comanche that might still be hiding among the sage, then returned to the sandy draw. They were quiet, moving slowly as they reloaded their rifles before putting them back in their scabbards or bedrolls. Sadness painted their faces as they looked at one another. Although they knew it was necessary, it was still the taking of life.

Estrella was the first to speak, "Since they took us, I thought many times about killing those men that took us. But..." she shook her head, unable to put her thoughts into words.

They breathed heavy, waiting for someone to say something about riding away or anything. As they leaned on their saddles, heads down, Bear licked Elly's hand and caused her to turn, just in time to see a smiling Reuben ride into the draw. He reined up and said, "Boy, was I glad to hear you start shootin'. I knew if they figured out there was only one of me, they would try to come at me from all sides and I'd be in a pickle! But when I heard those Henrys open up, I breathed easy!" He had stepped down and now stood beside Elly. He looked down at her, glanced to the others, and bent to kiss his wife, even as they watched.

They rode to the buttes, found a good arroyo, and

made camp for the night. It was too far back to the fort and the horses were tired. They had ample supplies and made a good meal and a cozy camp. It took a while for everyone to settle down enough to get some sleep, Reuben and Santiago taking turns at guard, but the night passed peaceably, and the morning came amidst a display of God's glory in full color, splashing the few remaining clouds with shades of pink, orange, and gold. When they rose from their blankets, the group was anxious to get on the trail and made short work of the return ride.

"Send this telegram to the governor, please," directed Reuben as he stood beside Elly before the counter in the telegrapher's office.

The man looked at Reuben, down at the paper and read the message,

> Governor Evans
> Denver, Colorado Territory
> Governor,
> Am in receipt of your telegram. We will spend the winter in our cabin in the mountains.
> When spring comes, we will go to South Park and begin our investigations.
> Reuben Grundy, Deputy Marshal
> Colorado Territory

"I ain't never sent a telegram to the governor before, but I remember the one you got. Are you sure you don't want to, uh, maybe, change this a mite? It seems to me that when the governor asks you to do somethin', a feller oughta be fer doin' it."

Reuben grinned, "We didn't ask for the job and we're not at his beck and call. If he doesn't like the answer, he can have the job." Reuben shrugged as the man stared at him, shook his head, and turned to begin tapping out his message.

With no need to wait for an answer they left the office, determined to finish getting ready to pull out and head home. It was still early; the sun was just painting the eastern sky and the few newly recruited soldiers were walking from the mess hall back to their barracks. Fort Garland had become little more than a recruitment station for the war that still waged in the east, and the garrison served as a way station. Understaffed as it was, the garrison at the fort was unable to fulfill their original mission of keeping peace with the natives and protecting settlers and any travelers that chose to take the old branch of the Santa Fe trail in either direction.

"I'm goin' to talk to the colonel, I'm sure he wants to know what happened with the Comanche, and I want to let him know we'll be leavin'. If you and Estrella will get your horses from the stables, I'll get mine and the pack animals after I talk with the colonel."

"Alright. We'll get our personal stuff packed and the rest laid out for the packs. But don't you take very long, we have a long way to go and there could be another storm anytime!" admonished Elly, giving a coy smile to her man. "And I am anxious to get home!" Reuben gave her a hug and turned to go to the commandant's office while she returned to their quarters for Estrella.

As he stepped into the outer office, the clerk behind the desk looked up, "Oh, Mr. Grundy, the colonel just asked me to fetch you." He motioned to the office door, "Go right in sir, he's expecting you."

The colonel looked up as Reuben stepped through

the door, "Mornin' Marshal, good to see you this morning."

"Colonel. The clerk out there said you wanted to see me?"

"Yes, right. I wanted to hear about your set-to with the Comanche, what happened?"

The colonel motioned for Reuben to be seated as he began to relate the confrontation with the Comanche. "After they killed the traders and stole the rest of the guns, I thought a time of reckoning was due, so..." he shrugged as he sat back in the chair.

"I spoke to Esquibel after you returned, and he was quite impressed with your commitment to make the Comanche pay for what was done. And as far as I can tell, you did a good job of balancing the scales. But..." he stood and went to his window, turned back, "I am being replaced. My orders are to take the new recruits east for training and the new commandant will be Lieutenant Colonel Samuel Tappan. It seems he is being disciplined by Colonel Chivington for a dust-up with some drunken natives." He paused, looking at Reuben, breathed deep and shrugged, "But I've been wanting to get in the fight, so this might be the answer."

"Good luck to you, Colonel. By the way, what's the word about the war?"

The colonel took his seat, put his elbows on his desk, clasped his hands and looked at Reuben. "The latest word is there was a grand battle at a place called Gettysburg. They're saying it was the biggest and bloodiest of all the battles. Some are estimating up to fifty thousand total casualties." He shook his head at the thought. "So I don't know how that can be called a victory, but apparently Lee retreated. General Meade lost a half-dozen of his top commanding generals and who knows how many more high-ranking officers, so there's certainly a need of officers." He paused again, looking down at his desk and lifted his eyes to Reuben. "Why aren't you in uniform, Grundy?"

Reuben let a slow smile split his face. "Oh, I was, Colonel. I was in it from the beginnin'. As a member of Berdan's sharpshooters, I saw more than my share of fightin'. Took several slugs myself and was mustered out because of it. Took me a while to recover. Lost my brother, and my family was killed by a gang callin' themselves the Home Guard."

The colonel looked at Reuben with a new respect. He had heard of the sharpshooters and knew they had gained considerable honor and notoriety, always at the front and the most effective of all units. For a man to serve and survive such fighting was extraordinary. He asked, "Is that what got you into the Marshal's service?"

"No, no. That's a different and very long story." He slapped his palms on the arms of the chair and stood. "So, if that's all you need me for, we're plannin' on pullin' out this mornin'. Goin' back home," nodding to the distant Sangre de Cristo range, "back over the mountains. We'd like to make it over the pass before too much more snow hits."

The colonel stood, extended his hand. "Good luck to you, Marshal. And," he dropped his eyes, looked back up and continued, "thanks for doing what we could not. Hopefully, your action against the Comanche will keep the peace for a while."

Reuben shook his hand, nodded, and turned to leave the office. He glanced back to see the colonel return to his window, probably thinking of his own circumstances and the uncertainty of his future. These were the thoughts of a man going to war, something he wanted, but now that it was a reality, he was reevaluating his motivation and aspirations.

———

THE BLAZING ORB WAS BLINDING AS IT SLOWLY ROSE ABOVE the mountains to the east. The bright lances of gold bent over the peaks to splash their color and light across the vast expanse of the San Luis valley. With only a single thin wisp of a cloud in the western sky, the azure canopy welcomed the morning and looked down upon the three travelers. Each rider trailed a pack horse, panniers newly loaded with fresh supplies from the post sutler. Ammunition, material, hardware, trade goods, and even seeds, both flower and vegetable, an expressed desire of Elly to have some semblance of a garden and flowers to make their cabin a home.

Reuben led the group, Elly close behind followed by an anxious Estrella. For the first time in a long time, the girl was able to dream and hope about a future that held mysterious promise, but promise, nevertheless. After her time as a captive that had robbed her of any hope, it was pleasant to consider what might be and what she might become. Elly had spoken to her about her life with them, and the possibility of a life of her own with a man of her choice, a life that could include children and many other possibilities. She rode the palomino that she had begun calling Missy because of her sometimes-sassy ways and trailed the other palomino that now served as a pack horse, that had been ridden by her friend, Goos. She smiled as she watched Elly and Reuben before her, the best friends she had known, and even good parental figures for her.

Elly was happy they were homeward bound, and with

a glance over her shoulder to Estrella, she smiled at the thought of having company that would be a member of the family. There had been many times when she missed the companionship of another woman, and having Estrella with them, would offer opportunities of both teaching and learning. She would be a good companion and friend, but no one could be a better friend than her husband. She smiled as she looked at the back of Reuben, who often turned to look back at them, always concerned about their welfare more than his own. She had a good life, not necessarily what she had dreamed of as a young girl, but in many ways more than she ever imagined.

Reuben was watching the trail before them, seeing Bear often stop and look back to be certain they were still following, and looking about them. The faces of the Sangre de Cristos were in their own shadow and would be until the sun was a little higher, but they were no less beautiful, an amazing display of the handiwork of the Creator. This was beautiful country, even the wide stretch of sage speckled flatlands that stretched to the north and west, framed by the distant San Juan Mountains. He smiled at the wonder of it all, thankful they were here in the mountains and away from the turmoil in the east where brother fought brother and neighbors killed one another. It was, in many ways, a senseless war. He considered them to be fighting for something that ought to be the right of every man, freedom. And both sides fought for their own ideas of what that freedom should be for others. He often thought that if they would just stop and think about it and be willing to grant to others what they desired for themselves, the war would quickly come to an end. He sighed heavily, shook his head slightly and shaded his eyes as he searched for the game trail they followed when they came this way, just a few days before.

To his right, just below the tree line, a grey line of a trail showed itself and he nudged his blue roan gelding, Blue, in that direction. He trailed the pack mule while Elly rode her leopard appaloosa mare and trailed the bay pack horse. He motioned to the women, pointing to the trail and said, "As soon as we get there, we'll take a short break, give the horses a breather and stretch our legs." Elly smiled, waved back, and relayed the message to Estrella. She knew this would be a two-day trip, but it was still a relief and pleasing to be homeward bound.

34 / HOME

When Reuben rolled from his blankets, he was surprised at the amount of snow that had fallen in the night. The storm came quietly and dropped its feathery flakes that stacked high all about them. As he flipped the blankets back, the motion stirred the downy whiteness and he wiped it from his face and shirt front. He shook his head as he dragged his wool frock uniform coat from beneath the blankets, shrugged into it and donned his wide brimmed hat. Climbing from the bedroll, he looked about the camp, saw the women still hunkered down into their blankets, their heads covered by the woolen covers, and snow piled on and about them. Bear had risen, shook the snow from his heavy coat, and stood waiting for Reuben for their early morning walk and survey of the territory.

With the Sharps slung muzzle down, on one shoulder, his small haversack with his bible and binoculars over the other shoulder, he started through the trees, careful to duck under the lower branches so as not to get a neck full of cold snow. They had rounded the southern point of the Sangres and made it to the foot of Mosca

Pass. He considered taking this pass, but preferred to return over the Medano pass, the same way they came before, familiarity being a comfort. Their camp was near the spring that had yet to freeze over and afforded them and the horses ample water for their camp and he was hopeful Elly would have some hot coffee waiting when he returned.

He took to the ridge just south of their camp, angling up the steep slope, slipping every now and then, he often had to use his hands to grab scrub oak or rocks to help his ascent. Once atop the ridge, he found a big rock beside some juniper and using his hat, swept it free of snow and took a seat, setting his haversack beside him and standing the Sharps on its butt and leaning against the rock beside his leg. Extracting his binoculars and bible, he looked around the many ridges that fell from the higher mountains, scanned the wide valley before him, the light snow still affording some visibility, all by the dim grey light of early morning, before opening the bible on his lap and searching for his scripture for the morning. He flipped the pages to Psalm 37 and began to read. As he came to verse 23, he paused, and began to read aloud as Bear looked up at him, mouth open, tongue lolling, but listening as if he understood. *The steps of a good man are ordered by the Lord: and he delighteth in his way. Though he fall, he shall not be utterly cast down: for the Lord upholdeth him with His hand.* He continued to read silently until he came to verse 27 and spoke aloud again, *Depart from evil, and do good; and dwell for evermore. For the Lord loveth judgment and forsaketh not his saints; they are preserved for ever: but the seed of the wicked shall be cut off.*

"Whew! That's some pretty heady readin', don't you think boy?" asked Reuben as he ran his fingers through Bear's scruff, chuckling as the dog leaned into his touch.

Reuben started his usual prayer, closed with his thanks, and with an amen, he lifted his eyes as the morning light began to crawl from over the mountains and shorten the shadows as the darkness over the valley retreated from the advancing light. He slipped his binoculars from the case, lifted them, and began searching the valley and nearby hills for any sign of life, friendly or otherwise. Seeing nothing but four legged creatures and a lot of white, he put the binoculars away, stood and slung the Sharps over one shoulder, the haversack over the other, and with a motion to Bear, started back to camp.

A thin tendril of smoke snaked its way toward the sky, dissipating into the overcast as it rose, and marked the site of their camp telling of the promise of his morning coffee. A smiling Elly greeted him as he walked through the stand of aspen, twisting side to side to make his way through the thick growth, and stepped close to the fire, taking his bride in his arms for the sugar to go with his coffee. Bear pushed against her leg, jealous of the attention and wanting his share.

It was just a short while later, they were on the trail, pushing past the sand dunes and searching for the trail of the Medano Pass. The dunes lay to the west of the trail, offering an unusual panorama for the travelers. The snow had been driven by the winds as if it were an artist painting the extraordinary landscape. Where the sand had been sculpted by the summer winds, the snow filled in the dips, draws, and scallops, making a tan and white optical treat. Each slope, hillock, and swooping draw provided an excuse to mutter an aww, oohh, or wow from those passersby that had never witnessed the hand of the Creator on this, His current canvas.

The trail bent away from the dunes, sneaking into the white-barked thickets of now naked aspen, clawing its way up the narrow draw that lay between the long ridges coming from the sky-scraping granite tipped peaks of the Sangre de Cristos. The tree cover made a good wind break from the incessant whistling and howling winds that carried snow to drift into and around the trees. The higher they climbed, the more they were forced to hunker deeper into their collars and grab for blankets for greater warmth. The horses bobbed and lowered their heads, trying to avoid the cold icicle like wind that searched for any vulnerability to stay the progress of the intruders to the mountain domain.

They made steady progress as they climbed up the narrow draw of the Medano Pass. To their left rose a long ridge that offered some protection from the high-altitude winds coming off one of the higher peaks of the range, rising about five hundred feet higher than the pass, its many finger ridges fed the wide draw with runoff come spring. Now the aspen and pine that littered the draw, gave sufficient cover to the travelers.

Since breakfast, they had made close to ten miles, but Reuben was determined to get over the pass before they stopped. He stood in his stirrups, shading his eyes and face with his hand, and searched the trail ahead. The cloud cover had settled over the mountains, dropping its skirts into the valleys and draws, and letting loose the heavy load of snow that filtered down with flakes almost the size of his palm. He turned in his saddle, looked back at Elly and Estrella strung out behind him, and lifted his voice so both could hear, "That snow is gettin' heavy! We need to keep movin' so we can clear the pass before we stop!"

Elly lifted her hand in a wave to show she heard and understood. She turned to look back at Estrella, "Did you hear?"

"Si, si. We need to keep going!" she answered, nodding. She nudged her palomino up the trail, pushing the bay pack horse closer to the appaloosa. Elly nodded, turned back to Reuben, and waved him on. Reuben settled into his saddle and slapped legs to Blue and the big roan stepped into the drifting snow, determined to make his way as his rider urged him onward.

As they neared the crest of the pass, the trail bent to the left, keeping in the cover of the tall ponderosa, but the wind was howling and whipping about, the big trees bending to its will and shaking their long-needled limbs to rid them of accumulated snow. As Reuben pulled his hat down even more, a big clump of snow dropped directly on his hat, covering his head and shoulders. Blue was startled and lunged forward, but the deep snow prevented any other response and the roan pawed at the deep drifts, busting through the snow that was more than belly deep.

The wind howled like a banshee, the icy snow cut any exposed flesh and the horses struggled with every step. Reuben tried hard to remember the distance to the crest where the trail made the last short climb over a saddle crossing, thinking it was only a mile from the bend. He felt Blue beginning to climb, and he peered out from his collars and the brim of his hat to see the round knob that marked the base of the 'S' curve climb to the crest. But the higher they climbed, the steeper the trail. Blue was struggling and Reuben slid down. With the snow waist deep, he flounced about, got his balance, and pushed ahead of Blue, breaking the trail for the tired animal. He held tight to the reins, fought the blowing snow, the deep drifts that sometimes showed to be almost chest deep, and he muttered a thanks that this was the first deep snow, and the drifts were soft. If it had been a late snow atop earlier drifts, the snowpack would be impossible to break through.

With the drifts broken, Blue and the mule following close behind, the trail for the women and their horses was considerably easier and when they broke over the crest and started down the west face of the mountains, the wind abated and came from behind. Once clear of the worst of the snow, Reuben swung back aboard and pushed on to the tree line. The sun filtered through the pine boughs, the wind had quieted, and the snow was behind them. They stepped down, loosened the girths on the horses, and grabbing up handfuls of dry grass, they wiped the horses dry, then let them stretch out and snatch up some grass for themselves. Once the horses were tended, the three dropped to the ground with the sun in their face and laughingly fell back, side by side, relief written on their faces.

After a short and relaxing break, they went to work to put together a hot meal. With some fresh cornmeal biscuits, venison strip steaks, and some timpsila, and of course the hot coffee, they were considerably refreshed and rested and anxious to get back on the trail. They were at the south end of the Wet Mountain Valley and started across the flats, crossing the creek and taking the trail that rode the shoulder of the foothills and stayed near the tree line of the juniper and piñon. The sun hung low in the southern sky as it made its arc from east to west, and it was starting to paint the bellies of the low hanging clouds in shades or orange and red when Reuben and company rode up the trail that crossed the saddle below their cabin. The leaf strewn trail that split off and climbed the slight rise into the trees beckoned the trio and when they rode into the clearing before the cabin, Reuben reined up, leaned his arms on the pommel, turned to Elly as she rode alongside, and with a broad smile said, "We're home!"

She laughed, shaking her head, and slid to the ground. She bounded up the steps and pushed open the door, turned and looked back as Estrella was climbing the steps of the porch, Bear at her side, and spread her arms wide, "We're home!"

Reuben laughed, stepped down and began stripping the packs and bedrolls, the saddles and other gear. He dropped everything into a big pile, took the leads of the six animals and started down the trail to the big meadow, knowing there was still ample grass for the animals, fresh water from the spring-fed creek, and shelter in the lean-to, but soon, with the worst of winter yet to come, he would need to make some improvements in the shelter and water supply.

He returned to the cabin, began packing gear and goods into the cabin, leaving some on the porch to be put away in the tack shed later. Once the pile was gone, he plopped down on the bench on the porch, looked around and with a broad smile, whispered, "We're home."

TAKE A LOOK AT: ESCAPE TO EXILE

STONECROFT SAGA BOOK ONE

AUTHOR OF THE BEST-SELLING BUCKSKIN CHRONICLES SERIES TAKES US ON AN EPIC JOURNEY IN THE NEW STONECROFT SAGA

It started as a brother defending the honor of his only sister, but it led to a bloody duel and a young man of a prominent family lying dead in the dirt...

Gabriel Stonecroft along with his life-long friend, Ezra, the son of the pastor of the African Methodist Episcopal church, at his side, the journey to the far wilderness of the west would begin. One man from prominent social standing, the other with a life of practical experience, are soon joined in life building adventures.

That journey would be fraught with danger, excitement, and adventure as they face bounty hunters, renegade Shawnee and Delaware Indians, and river pirates. The odds are stacked against the two young men that were lacking in worldly wisdom when it came to life on the frontier. But that reservoir of experience would soon be overflowing with first-hand involvement in happenings that even young dreamers could never imagine.

AVAILABLE NOW

ABOUT THE AUTHOR

Born and raised in Colorado into a family of ranchers and cowboys, **B.N. Rundell** is the youngest of seven sons. Juggling bull riding, skiing, and high school, graduation was a launching pad for a hitch in the Army Paratroopers.   After the army, he finished his college education in Springfield, MO, and together with his wife and growing family, entered the ministry as a Baptist preacher.

Together, B.N. and Dawn raised four girls that are now married and have made them proud grandparents. With many years as a successful pastor and educator, he retired from the ministry and followed in the footsteps of his entrepreneurial father and started a successful insurance agency, which is now in the hands of his trusted nephew. He has also been a successful audiobook narrator and has recorded many books for several award-winning authors. Now finally realizing his life-long dream, B.N. has turned his efforts to writing a variety of books, from children's picture books and young adult adventure books, to the historical fiction and western genres which are his first love.

CPSIA information can be obtained
at www.ICGtesting.com
Printed in the USA
LVHW010323090322
713002LV00006B/223